A Message from the Author:

Thanks for taking your time out and your well hard-earned money to support me in my journey on yet another wonderful novel. During this crazy pandemic, we must find the positive even in the most negative of life situations or shall I say finding the best in the toughest of test. Remember that you could have been in some hospital at this very moment on someone's ventilator.

Love one another, meaning wear a mask, not only to protect yourselves. But as well as to protect others too. Be considerate and also mindful sometimes you must think for others. Just like when you are driving a car in everyday life. You must not only focus on the way you drive. But also pay attention to the way others drive. So, you can prevent an accident even if the person behind the wheel of their vehicle is not focus or under the influence. The difference could be life or death. This is the same way you all should take precaution with covid and wash your hands every 30 to 50 minutes, wear a mask covering when you are out handling business the difference can be life or death.

We have the name united states and but yet how come when it comes to fighting this virus together, we are divided people. We need to stand together as one, we supposed to be the land of the free, but why we do not' live by that creed. Black lives do matter but guess what all people of color live matter. If we would work as one, we could not have to wait on a cure or vaccine people. Many people have lost their lives.

Even small children let us not only to stick together in the Olympics or new years' time when we are waiting on the ball to drop. Do not aid this animal of a virus to take your life or anyone else lives for that matter. I do not' know about you but I do not want my children or I to become just another death statistic. Remember we are the brave America ladies and gentlemen we are number one, second to non-red, white, and blue!

I love all of you and encourage all of you to help someone else other than yourselves. As for my African Americans we stand for our rights and stand for our children of tomorrow's generation. We have lost many to the hands of dirty officers or just those who are racists who do not like us for whatever reasons we protest for the right to be treated as equal brothers and sisters. We do not protest to be breaking into people stores and homes. It solves nothing setting fires to our own people businesses. How those of you that do this is not any better than The Dirty police officers or better than those who locked down on us a wrong is wrong no justification people.

Last but not least with certainly not least those of you that have goals go after them do not take no for an answer when you find the opportunity. Go hard, make those who past you by or did not believe in you make them regret, for the ones who turned their backs on you make them take a second look.

Stay focus by surround yourself with those who would like to see you succeed in everything you touch. Perfect your craft and take full advantage of every day. That opens never settle achieve and reach for greatness. "" Who Am I?" I am just a guy people counted out, who is now Best-Selling Author! I was not supposed to be here.

Acknowledgements:

WOW! Is all I can say. I am blessed to be in the best of health and doing what I love to do yet again with another outstanding Jay Phoenix Novel. Truly all praise is do unto the highest the most merciful God is truly Good!

I thank him first for my life, the air in my lungs and I also thank him for my talents, my shirt comings and the hunger that burns deep down inside of me. I live by (Hard work Dedication) something I've learn from the Best ever boxer Floyd money Mayweather. If you apply this in everyday work ethic. You will surely get results because hard work pays. Just like practice makes perfect.

To me it is highly important to convey the same energy from novel to the next novel. Despite the type of novel, I choose to do or category/genre I bring it out of. I thank God for my ability to be creative and write any kind of novel. Something most good authors cannot do. So, I am very thankful for being so versatile, blessed with an open mind.

(Thank you, God for a Gift!)

Now I like to give just a few special thanks. I would like to thank my mother who gave me the idea of becoming an author anyhow. God bless her soul. I miss you super Queen.

To my sister Doris, I love you and thank yo of believing in your young brother. Get Well Soon. Also, special shoutout to Iesha, you had my back for many years. You even have my name tatted on you. 101 I am flattered, and we will always be close. Remember I love you when nobody else in this world does. Be strong Queen life has it is up and down. God will not put more on you than you can bare.

To my loving and supportive friends, Big Loo, Straight Hood Mike, and Billy Joe, also trying not to forget those who deserve my love and shout out. Also, special thank you to Tiandreia, Joe Singletary, Ashely Monique, my boys LOD, Traebands and Aron. To Topie for being sweet and supportive. Thanks Ma I cannot forget my Tar Heels sister Gloria Brazil Hill and someone who been around before I was ever signed Judith. I have a lot on my team of support system. I consider some fans, friends, and family. All of you guys' words of advice or encouragement has all been like extra fuel to my fire. So, I do not' forget loyalty, something we Leo's are strong. Not to mention that we oozed the confidence as well.

Thank you to Michelle, Kenyada B, as well Myra G much love to you and words really do not need to beside to Tinesha you been one of my biggest cheerleaders. I appreciate you through two decades of love. Shoutout to Christa, Annette, as well l as Yasemeen and my BFF Tinesha. To Kenyada you keep being an awesome mother to your children. You are strong black queen and I appreciate the way you back me and enjoy my work, continue to wear your crown the world sees the strength.

Last but certainly not forgotten to my Home Team at Divinity Publishing LLC, for making this all possible once again. My loyalty lies here. This the te4am I play for leaving a mark. The opportunity has been like a football handed off to me. I am the running back and no fumbles I am running my ass off. Completing touch down after touchdown (GAME ON!) I work hard 24/7

-365. I am never off, and I don't sleep I won't stopped. I thank you all for seeing me as a fine prospect and back me.

As for my publisher Elaine, you are a remarkable person and a good mother, but a true definition to the word friend too. Thanks for seeing my ideas and vison, as well as my creativeness. When I step to the office your all ears and back my plans. You do not' try to harness my talent, love you for that. I appreciate all you do.

For those of you who counted me out or did not believe in me or ever doubted the GOAT. Do not trip LOL It is mind over matter. Because I mind because you do not' matter.

To my many fans, family, and friends you all enjoy this Jay Phoenix Novel!!

Table of Contents

Prologue

Prologue

Robert Harold and his newfound date Amanda were all over one another, In the back seat of his dark tinted window limousine The older mafia Boss Harold was enjoying Himself. As This bad Russian beauty stroked His Penis In a back-and-forth motion. As He To head back without a Worry In the world, there was stuck on He had no shame in Cheating on his lovely wife. The man was selfish but He was the Boss, At mad man, and Leader of the Harold Mafia He own clubs and Businesses up and down the East coast of t united states, like His father back In the This bite was Just as lethal and a reach that was very long.

"MMmmmm" she moaned As Amanda Spit on to his dick for extra lubricated watched Her Saliva trickle down His Shaft and the length of Roberts's pole "Shit why do you like to tease me so much Baby? Robert asks. As he began kissing her red lipstick lips passionately. She continued her strokes speeded up the pace just a bit. "Because I no American Bitch, I aim to please and o things my way." She smiled. Her heavy Russian accent turns him on more. Robert Harold had yet to have sex with Amanda, she had given him some oral sex a couple of times since the night they first met at a mutual friend's white party. In Buffalo New York. Tonight, as agreed upon was supposed to be the first time Robert would get to be inside of her. He had known her for about a month now and being impatient was getting the best of him. Amanda was fully aware of Robert Harold being married; she could care less. Amanda had talked Robert into crossing the border into his enemy's territory of Canada. Canada was controlled by the most dangerous group known to many as the Generation. All of the Canadian cartels ran by their ruthless leader over the decades Sylvester Maccin. Robert Harold took a gamble in the middle of a war. Sneaking over into his rival territory just for sex.

Amanda had told him that she wanted their first time to be someplace high above ground level. This is when she suggested one of Toronto Ontario's famous tourist attractions the CN Tower. Canada's most recognizable and celebrated icon, defining the drive Toronto skyline. At 55.33m (1,815 ft 5in). located in downtown Toronto with 147 floors, truly a breathtaking landmark.

Amanda was very a4ttractive standing at around 5.8, very curvaceous she had a shaved haircut that put you in the mindset of that girl in G.I. Jane, (Demi

Moore). Twenty-six years of age well that was what the women had told Robert Harold. He was weak for younger women and a sucker for weakness. He had never once questioned or had his goons check out Amanda Dupri's story or run a background check on her identity. Not even so much as her fingerprints were run for a background check. It would become a costly mistake for the leader of the Harold Mafia. Amanda wore a red maxi long dress with slits on both sides' revealing just a little bit of her well-toned legs, with some red peep toe stiletto pumps. She was very smart not allowing Robert to reach between her thighs so he would discover the pistol position she had taped to her thigh.

The Russian Assassin played her role well. She was loyal to the core and had put her life on the line plenty of times for Sylvester and the Canadian cartel. No spring chicken, she was a true soldier. Olga was her name, and Amanda was her alias, that she used when associated with the Harold Mafia.

Two dark tinted windowed SUVs drove closely behind Robert Harold's limousine. As one SUV led the way down Bremner Blvd to the CN Tower. Each SUV was filled four deep with Harold's mafia best goons. Robert Harold kept nothing but the elite best on his payroll. Those men did their job to perfection protecting Robert his wife and his children. All Robert Harold could think about was going up into Amanda's wall raw. She told him she like it rough, and he was ready to deliver. The ride on the elevator up to the top lasted a few minutes. But felt like a lifetime to Robert Harold. As he got tired of his wife blowing up his cell phone, so he placed it on silent. He did not need to be disturbed. Soon as the duo reached the top of the CN Tower, Robert Harold was all over Amanda like white on rice. "MMmmmm Hhhmmm this should be a good fuck underneath the nightly sky." She knew her partner Tarbaby was listening in on their earpiece. She had just poked in code. Letting her partner know that she had Robert Harold in position. Amanda made sure to keep Robert Harold's back turned in the direction the bell 430 helicopter all red was approaching from. It never raised his suspicion as to why she was removing her red stiletto pumps. Robert had managed to free one of her breasts from her dress. He was sucking on her nipple. "Yes, Baby don't stop!" Amanda moaned out loudly. All the while reaching for her gun from the thigh holster. "Don't worry I'm going to fuck the shit out of your Russian slut." He uttered. Robert ever notices what was unfolding, lust had clouded his judgment, as it had done to many powerful leaders in history past. His goons on the grown looked up when they saw the huge hovering copter around the roof of the CN tower. One by one the men took off running. Several of them that was guarding the towner entrance made their way to the elevator. In hopes the cold makes it up to the roof on time, deep down they knew the ride up to the top would take forever. Tarbaby lowers the step ladder down from the chopper. Amanda held the back of Robert Harold's head. Pushing him or them onto her breast like an anew born breastfeeding baby. "POP! POP!" she let off two shots Robert Harold immediately collapsed to the cold roof floor. Amanda covered up her breast. She was relieved to finally have stopped his dirty old hands from touching her body. Garbling on his blood, Robert Harold's chest heaved up and own. "By the way my name is Olga! I am no man's slut, PRICK!!" with that said she fired one last round into Robert Harold's forehead. Her dress resembled water, from the wind of the helicopter. It delivered a ripple effect. "Move! Move! Move!" the door flew open. As Robert Harold soldiers began firing shots. Olga took off running toward the ladder. She leaped and grabbed pulling herself up, she smiled. "Ya okay, my lady?" Tara asked as they flew away into the night!

G FOR GENERATION

WELCOME TO
G FOR GENERATION

A Canadian Mafia Story

1ST OF A TRILOGY

By: JAY PHOENIX

Chapter One

Joel of Generation Intelligence team had made all of the Necessary Arrangements for the meeting between the Two most Hated families, bitter rival for many years. Sylvester leader of the Notorious *Generation* aka known to some as the Canadian Cartel wanted to Expand Territory. A line his father put in place years ago when he won the war running Harold mafia Organization out of Canada.

But it was now Sylvester who wanted to make money In the United States. But on the east coast Where the Entire coast belonged to The Harold Mafia.

It was early at nine o'clock am, as not to me people were up and starting their day on this particular Sunday morning at the small park. There were a few people getting in their early morning jogging exercise in, as some all-Black Tinted windows SUV's Pulled up. One would have thought the president was in town. People in the park looked and out of curiosity until they saw several men in tuxedo's jumpsuits jumped out of the vehicles armed carrying assault rifles and handguns noticing this person scattered like mice from fire. pandemonium as people ran all different directions, nearly breaking their necks to get out of the harm's way. as the leader of the *Harold Mafia Family*, Robert Harold Sr., stepped out of one of the SUVs. if there's a couple guys attempted to escort him to the park bench, but Robert Harold Sr., dismissed it because he saw that his enemies Sylvester men was falling back in distance from their meeting place. So he had his men do the same, it was agree upon that it would be a harmless business meeting. No guns amongst the two men. no violence just two bosses. "Hello" Sylvester said, as he sat on the park bench feeding the birds bead crumbs. He never turned around to acknowledge Robert, it was like eyes when the back of his head. Sylvester was on this turf of Canadian soil. The man no worries, he said, cool, not at all feeling threatened. Its confidence gave him strength and his strength gave him power was deep, deep pockets, Sylvester has plenty of resources and usually what he wanted he gets.

No handshake was exchange it was no love at all both me and hated one another. It supposed to continue to watch Lake Ontario and feed the birds. To the seat on the small bench as well. His dark shades made him resemble Ray is Robert Harold senior dressed in all white. The cocaine white tuxedo adjusted his next time he looks apart and look stream the shark so that is it was just a little bit older than him but both men were African Americans just from different countries. "Hello, is very unexpected I was saying my friend, but we wait for not phony bosses." Robert stated, "Exactly Robert, so I will get to the point I want to set up clubs on the east coast and also start a couple of casinos in South Beach Miami and in Cherokee North Carolina. "Sylvester tone was serious and left no room for negotiating to remove this Shades rubber cleared his throat "are you insane?" You know the rules are father said years ago why should I allow you to eat off my territory Sylvester? Robert, ask you to get a bit upset.

"What the fuck you mean! You do not allow anything with me I take what I want I could have just crossed the line without a meeting. But my wife feels like shit show you a little respect make no mistake what I allow you is to breathe."

Robert jumped up from the seat "you threatened me ", Robert Harold guns me noticed things were our farm looking like she was about to hit the fan if I never moved from his spot, you are not even looking at Robert is ahead of the Canadian cartel pulled out a thirty-eight special and placed the gun on his lap. Sylvester continues to sit like he was on vacation he had a Raptors t-shirts saying we Noah no you all ain't in the men wore blue jeans with Jordans on his feet and I wrapped it all black logo fitted cap that he had drunk no light above his eyes. you would have thought he was a young typical thug. "You muthafucka, you lied." Robert eyed the gun on Sylvester's lap, "There no rules in wars and no respect amongst enemies," He stated Robert knew Sylvester was right. Sylvester only had three goons in the distance with him, his ace in the hole was his own gun. He could kill or take Robert Harold hostage, and no one could do nothing about it. At this moment Robert Harold Sr wished he had allowed the meeting to be held on his home tour or Buffalo New York. "I will give you to Sunset today to give me an answer and then I declare war. do not be stubborn my move would not hurt your pockets. but a war would choice is yours Robert. With that said Sylvester put his gun back inside of the news aper beside him to conceal and he tucked it underneath his armpits and stood walked away. Leaving Robert Harold feeling like a bitch. He was caught off balance on his heels not on his toes. To start something there at the moment would be suicide with a lot of consequences. He and His group of soldiers would not even make it across the border if he touched Sylvester now. The man had entire country

behind him. But Robert knew he would not call, and he would not back down
he would win the war.

Twenty-Seven years Ago!!!

The rival between generation and Harold mafia was legendary like crips and bloods before far worse it all started with Monroe Harold relocated his Harold mafia to Canada version of New York City Toronto ON. having Buffalo and the entire East Coast was not good enough he had no idea how strongly in powerful Simon Maccin head with him leading the Canadian Cartel when toes was stepped on Simon Maccin was not one to take losses. So he gave him a row a chance to leave Canada for good or his hand will be compelled the warning was ignored and a war broke out like no one had ever seen it was about chess moves not checkers at all who was the most ruthless leader and who wanted to be down in the history books as a family everyone feared Simon Maccin, Sylvester father went to the extraordinary extremes as news stations worldwide not just CBC had reports daily of the balance taking place in Canada it was truly Ground Zero it wasn't about just who owned business or whomever turf nor who could sell the most product and keep the junkies hungry but power in demise bragging rights were at stake assignment orders his goons to deliver nothing but head shots children were no exceptions being killed then hung from light poles when the sunrise people cry their eyes out it was seen from a horror film members of the Harold mafia mothers and wives were brutally beaten by pipes leaving little chance for open caskets salmon wonder war and in line was drawn until now!

Chapter Two
Virginia Motel

Sonya Maccin was a lovely, beautiful woman. Nate loved everything about her from her hips and apple bottom booty to Her waist had to be a twenty-six, and her ass had to be around the forty-two department, she did not have one breast, But He was the descendant with her picture-perfect body, Sonya and Nate had been Sneaking around behind her father's back for about ten months now. Now do not get me the wrong. He knew Sylvester Maccin Was a dangerous man overprotective of his only daughter Sonya. Hell, iF knew Nate was fucking his daughter on a regular, Nate would've even dead a long time ago. But, when he wanted something or someone, he Stopped at nothing Nate was persistent if nothing else. seer his Big brother Desmon was the same way, Sylvester was his Boss, he had been working for him for a good eight years. As well as this only family win brother Desmon. Nate always looked up to Sylvester and been loyal. Because he had been like a father to his brother and him Ever since he had taken then in off the Streets, Desmon and Nate had no food, and their only shoes were hard me downs. His brother and him had 'No home and no education, their mother Sindel was a straight up Junkie, who never gave a damn about Desmon and Nate. Shit, Nate could not tell nobody nothing about their father, because he never ever met their sorry Son of a bitch. Nate was twenty-four now and If He ever met him, he would gladly Spit In his face, Air him out, and burry the bastard Personally!!! Call it hate and wrong. Nate called it real and right.

As Nate laid flat out on his back in the small motel room, watching Television in His boxers. "Baby," Sonya Stepped out of the bathroom from taking a shower. They had an intense love making Session not even 45 minutes ago, Shit Nate's erection was still stiff from that Smacking pussy, so Sonya just put on him. Sonya had shoulder length, Jet black silky hair, with a couple of blond highlight Streaks, Nate was mesmerized by her beauty. The towel she had wrapped around her waist. barely covered her ample ass cheeks, As She sat down onto the bed, drying her hair with Another towel. So, you got Jokes?" Nate questioned. Sonya Snickered. Looking over her shoulder at Nate. "What Are you talking about Nate! ", Can't a girl get herself I freshened up to head back to Campus? She doubled question, 'Sure you can, But Why you gotta tease me, half naked and shit you know you got me on fire," He grinned, "NO, NO!", She Sang like that Destiny she song. "Boy we are done for today my pussy is already Sore and I gotta be back on campus by 10:00pm, so Tell MR hard on to get some.

rest" she said as She licked her lips Seductively, while eyeing hard on. Before He could reply, Sonya looked over at His 'flagpole Nate WAS completely Exposed, stroking it gently, Sonya reached over with her left hand and squeezed and a massaging His dick, as Nate removed His hand and the back to let his girl work her magic. Nate knew that she would not leave him blue balls. Even though he had beat that pussy up numb! Sonya still had those full Sexy lips NATE loved so much. Nate moaned as He felt her Warm tongue running Swirls and circles around the tip of his manhood. "Damn I love the taste of your dick daddy' she confessed. Suck that

dick then he commands, Nate pushed Down on the back of her head as He could not take that teasing Shit no longer. "Slurp! "Slurp! Slurp! was all you could hear throughout the room, the one the wetness of Sonya's mouth on his manhood. He combed His hands through Sonya's long damped hair. As it tangled around 'Nate fingers, He controlled the pace and picked up the speed, Sonya had NATE boxer is and the Sheets underneath him all wet up. Home girl Spit and Slobber His knob well. "ALL DAT ' he said in a matter of Seconds me Sonya, Sonya baby. Here it comes and in one swift motion, she deep throated his dick and Let Him coat the back of her throat, As She Swallow every last drop. NATE grunted in Pleasure, and now all wet up Sweat up, NATE was in need of a shower, he hated the fact Sonya had to get back to Virginia Tech where she was enrolled at. But they did understand the Job was to make sure she was safe, Because her. father at Boss, had declared war, And Sylvester knew Sooner or later

intelligence team in form a Robert of Sonya attending Virginia Tech. In mind, Sylvester was being inconsiderate of those He loved and cared for, He was putting his entire family at risk Sonya and his wife Ajah Maccin Had no idea of the danger and threat

surrounding them 24/7. Sonya Jumped up and down to fit into her Jeans, NATE had sent His Brother Desmon a text message. What is up for tonight? Des had left the room for a while to give Sonya and Nate Privacy Nate was glad Sonya had promised her daddy Just two more weeks, and she would head back to Canada. until the war was over with. No matter how crazy it may sound, Sylvester always let his daughter have her Way "okay Nate ready to go. Sonya Shouted breaking his train of thought, Shit He was still half naked.

Maccin Estate, Toronto Ontario

The west wing Conference room was packed with the heavy hitters of The Generation family. Everyone has waiting patiently for their leader and Boss to enter the conference room to speak on the WAR at hard, Sylvester was never on time. He always set up meetings with his family and told all of them never to be late, Sylvester Maccin loved to make people wait on him. He knew without him the show will not go on. And He was right understanding his position of power. All of Sylvester Cid's admired him and loved him. Especially his little princess he liked to call her. His one and only daughter Sonya, Sonya was currently under the protection of Nate and Desmon down in Virginia. But Sylvester had summoned Desmon up to Toronto for this meeting Damon, Sylvester's oldest son, was in deep thought at the Conference table, most paying any attention to Olga and Iceberg argue about usually nothing. Big Iceberg was just as his name was, because he was larger than life Standing at 289 pounds and 5.11 easy, when the Canadian walk by you, you could literally see his shadow swallow you up. Iceberg was not black as TAR Babu. But he was close enough, Iceberg was Sylvester's bodyguard for

Some reason The Russian beauty Olga and him could never co-exist in any room young Damon was always worried about his father, because he knew his father was an important man and always had a target on his chest, because there was always up and coming motherfucker's who wanted to take over. Damon had always stood back and watch his father win war after was there but never a war as big as This one, and problem with that this particular war was father was the wrong one in the one trying to entire take over to the east Coast. That belonged to the Harold mafia for years now.

Damon and the entire conference room was interrupted. As the young Chinese maid open the door for The Boss Sylvester Maccin and an unknown stranger walking behind him. As they enter the coffee aroma Conference room, As The gentleman took their seats at the Conference table, everyone eyed the bronze skin complexion big man. With a scar on his temple of his head, Olga licked her lips Lustfully as she eyed the Stranger down, Desmon was the only one at the table who knew who the stranger was only because Sylvester had been called him about the America man, but He would link up with to carry out a mission. "You guys I am sorry to be late, but business is always on my clock, Sylvester Said. As he saw the uneasiness on everyone around the large conference table, He cleared his throat as he continues. "Family let me put all of your curiosity to rest. This American man sitting to the left of me. Is Gauge, you guy's will treat him with the same love and loyalty you have shown me. "I welcome this man into my home and into my Generation. Our generation and I want you guys to welcome him with open arms." Guage was recently locked up in the state of South Carolina with my youngest son Smurf, and to make a long story short. He saved Smurf from a possible earth. So, I owe this man my life." Guage interrupted Sylvesterr, not know this was something you did not due to Sylvester. Sylvester knew that Gauge was still green to the rules. "Mr. Sylvester, you owe me nothing. I did what I had to do and I "his sentence was cut short. When he saw Sylvester wave him of and shook his head. "I said I owe you my life and that's final." Sylvester challenged but no one dared to open their mouths.

Guage studied the eyes of everyone around the table he could sense no one trusted him. But he could understand why These people did not know him as of yet. Sylvester took a sip of his water because unlike everyone else, he hated coffee. "Well then Gauge, Welcome to the Generation, my brother." Everyone around the table said in unison 'Welcome to the Generation!" Gauge nodded his head to everyone, as he eyed the only women at the large circular table. Who was staring at him not only curiously but also lustfully? Gauge return the stare and let it know that she would get to know him personally. Sylvester noticed the heated stare between the two and cleared his throat. "Now I will introduce you to your new family Gauge, across from me sits my oldest son, Damon. You have met my youngest son Smurf, But Damon heir is the heir to my empire." Damon nodded his head to acknowledge Gauge. But remained silent as he studied the huge African American man. "And this here Jamaican to my far left is Tarbaby." Sylvester pointed in to Tarbaby direction. Tarbaby, greeted nice to meet ya!" as he flashed all mouth full of gold teeth. "Same to you," Gauge said. Sylvester continued, 'this is this is no other than my bodyguard iceberg, date in the message stand they both was extremely large but in the he is their leader man was back in the latest seine the bear was moved by each other and I am the

G FOR GENERATION

Russian beauty proudly announced impatiently Sylvester gave it by chuckle yes I'm sorry my dear days this year is over my head Gator yes don't let her beautiful you many men and women have fallen victim to her hands supposed to stay here I see it's a pleasure to meet you page smirked likewise Ogle wade with a smile date again I will help you and in mired the fact that underneath all that beauty she was still a deadly woman at heart assassin creed who was not to be underestimated gave toggle bolt new there's stairs that they both would get to know one another on a more personal level later now ask what happens this is this street sine who to win that you will be working with him down in the southern parts of the state the two parameters changed theirs and both being gay a slight nod of acknowledgement is a sign of respect.

Sylvester continued, Desmon will have your back at all times, and you will have his a well. Sylvester gave a stone-cold serious stare." That is my word, which is all the man he is his word, other than his nut sack. The entire table laughed at Sylvester sense of humor the box of generation stood to his feet family I have summoned you all today because I have declared war the lines have been drawn generation stand for what it wants no if ands nor what about it quit indeed this Canadian cartel over the years has seen its share of wars but none that serious and deadly as the opposing family. The Harold mafia Robert Harold senior would not back down as easy as our past enemies Sylvester took a sip of his ice cold water before he continued I love you all as my own flesh and blood but in war there are no room for emotions nor love we should show no mercy on our oldest rival Harold mafia no remorse one by one we will take over every state on the East Coast until the United states belong to us we will turn their turf in two hours we will spare no one at all whomsoever shares Harold senior bloodline will die "Do I make myself clear?" Sylvester questioned the entire conference room in unison everyone shouted yes Sir as if they I was a part of the Canadian or American army good all I can say is that when it's settled we will have the victory I hope to see every one of your face is alive and well to celebrate this victory with me so versus candy entire conference table he pause for mom to see if he sends any weaknesses in his family as he studied each and every one size pleased with his answer of nothing but Lord soldiers he continued as he pays back and forth but hands behind his back in a parade rest fashion." now first I will hit the pockets of the best Robert Harold gave you and Desmond will take Tennessee South Carolina Florida and Georgia and of course Virginia when my daughter Sonya is that I want y'all to protect with your life." I will contact young Nate to assist you to Olga I want you and time baby to head over to New York and Philadelphia I will send a few soldiers with you guys to aid what I need done iceberg and myself have other business to handle when all of you reach your destination's contact me ASAP but further instructions you are all dismissed Sylvester walked out and told his son Damon to follow him everyone exit the conference room to carry out their mission that had been sprinkled upon them gazing over bold wishing that Sylvester had put them together on the mission of their own.

Sylvester's office

Ajah Maccin And Sylvester had been married for 24 years the Switzerland woman never asked him for his match only that he put his blood family before any and everything so that's I had always been real hard on his youngest son Smurf it was as he treated Sonja and Damon as his favorites and Smurf was always the black sheep of the family he brought the Mac and family all kinds of shame and embarrassment when Smurf was in junior high school that's when the trouble began the boy hated how other kids wouldn't hang with him nor play games with him reason for this was that all his classmates parents had warned their children not to hang around Smurf all because his daddy was a mobster who killed women and children it didn't matter all the rumors were true and Sylvester was a cold hearted man that really showed love to anyone only his wife are Jamaican and his only daughter Sonia got his real love he loved his voice too but he always told Damon a Smurf the man up it broke his wife heart when he refused to free his younger son from prison Sylvester said ,"Ajah That boy has been hard headed and trouble from the beginning and now we'll let him learn the lessons Smurf was sentence to 12 years in a South Carolina state prison

Ajah Megan was 42 years of age she was still very attractive for her age the long-haired Switzerland bombshell kept her health and body up very well she still turned heads whenever she was in public area without knowing Ajah stormed into her husband's office without knocking. He was in the middle of discussing some business with their son Damon so there is a student to his feet and gave his wife a heated disapproving stare as Damien watched she said we need to talk right now Sylvester so first I gave his son a light nod or the head

Damon stood hugged his mother and exited the office as Ajah smiled. "your son is on his way home and you need to show him some fatherly love when he gets here Ajah the man did how so baby he asked something about early release here the boy has done there his whole sentence he was under four years to go anyway she said with hands on her diamond shaped hips that's good married and I will have a lot of last time to make up and I don't need you telling me what to do he said in a very serious tone Ajah came around his desk and hugged her soulmate Sylvester I just want you to treat him like our other children can you promise that Ajah questioned anything for you sweetheart as he kissed her the first lady of the streets lips smurfing I will let bygones be back bygone's thank you Sylvester as she turned to leave the office Ajah had a smirk on her face she always got her way.

Chapter Three
Memphis Tennessee

Club rotten apple was literally off the charts every one of their Mamas was up in the joint DJ 3000 kept the music in funky beats flowing like a river several players from the Tennessee Titans was in attendance buying Our Lady drinks straight out of VIP closed off section club right in the apple had an upper deck and a lower section downstairs as well upstairs was where the private rooms were located Ballers and bitches get their freak on regularly upstairs. This was no strip club spot but let us face it every club needed private rooms like rotten apple, because after dancing and bumping all up on some big booty right Schmitt you'll be waiting to freak right there on the spot not wanted to wait to get to a hotel or your crib club right apple was one of the many clubs owned and ran by Harold mafias family Mr. Robert Harold Sr himself a place his young trigger man in charge of the club he went by the name of BLOW reason being he was a trigger happy motherfucker, who didn't hesitate to blow your brains out and read the number two he earned the nickname below was because he loved that loud pack lo literary was blowing his lungs away the man was only 28 and had been spoken weed for as long as he could possibly remember damn boy stayed has a kite but he ran the riding apple to perfection though had been running with Mr. Harold mafia for about 9 to 10 years he was lowered to the core and what did anyone who had beat with his well respected mentor and boss Robert Harrell senior every once in a while below was ordered to handle some St beef but nothing major anymore since his position in the family moved up the promotion made his job easier to just babysitter club in his hometown and he made more paper now than he did when he was a field soldier below miss being away from the action inflicting pain on people but he rolled with the position he earned below had the club rocking as mad women feel the club there had to be at least 10 letters for every one man blow smiled to himself as he looked at the crowd from far at the bar he locked eyes with his DJ 3000 he gave him a slight head not to the big fella and DJ 3000 gave the thumbs up as he dropped a current booty hit song named clappers as his ladies went ballistic some ran from the bar grabbed the man onto the dance floor and went to work back in their booty's up and making their juice around booties clap the beat generated through the club the atmosphere was stupid and off the chain.

"Yo, bump my nigga, see the bitches is we got up in here tonight?" Blow asks his bartender Bump. As he scanned the crowd back and forth combing his eyes through the selection of women so he could decide who he would take upstairs to blow her back out. mum was an old school brother in his mid-fifties he was a black man who had seen it all and been through it all none of the females really faced him his name was Bob because his face was literally covered with bumps blow always told him that he needed try that proactive stuff the people be showing on television commercials.

"Yo Younger I see some bad hunters in the spot tonight but required SC Ford the lovely lady it is by drink and gave her a warm smile the job at the ripe apple as a bartender was just bumped part time job his day job was at the bowling alley down the street. "Damn right old timer, I'm a get ya laid with one of those young bitches tonight." Blow shouted over the loud music excitedly. Not even giving a damn that the young lady was still sitting at the bar sipping her drink and being all ears. The red bone cute face body banging but her girls was out on the floor clapping their cheeks all on a nigga dick. She herself was left alone and like I always feeling insecure she had no other entertainment, so she put her ears in the field Mr. bump add his young Fran end balls down because I always told below to stop calling women bitches, this bitch or bitch that. "Listen son, most of these ladies are young enough to be my daughter hell even granddaughters besides, I am a happily married man of 27 years and I'm just fine where I'm at blow rolled his eyes as he lit a cigarette and inhaled the smoke and why can't you stop calling the latest bitches. Is that the price word your Mama taught you as a kid old school Bump double question?

I don't know where before block they respond the female was caught both the attention you tell them Mr. Blow niggers these days ain't gotta respect for a sister the Big Block chick at the bar found this spoke up and now made her presence be known Blow, blew out of cloud of smoke into the Big Block this direction Mr. Bump dropped his head because he knew his young friend had bad temper. "Nosey bitch!" we did not ask your opinion that is why your fat is occur as alone now at the bar you talk to fucking much below shouted angrily the girl mouth fell open speechless as now on the verge of tears blood never took numbers of the two guys walking into the direction, but below right-hand man Patrick saw what was unfolding before his eyes.

"Fuck you Nigga!" Big Block chick yelled as she stood to her feet to leave, she snapped her neck back into Blow and Mr. bumps direction. "Nigga you gone get served believe that." The Big Block threating in an accent Blow could not quiet figure out where he heard it before from. "BITCH" he withdrew his pistol off his waistline. "You are threating me in my club?" He questioned in full rage. The girls' eyes almost popped out of her sockets. She had heard about the notorious gangsta and how he took n bullshit now she was in same shit with that nigga. Before Blow could finish yelling at Big Block or aim his weapon. He heard "Blow watch out!" Blow was quick on his feet and quicker on his toes as he recognized that voice to be his main man, Patrick. Blow heed the warning as he did not even turn around to look, He grabbed his first shield who as old man Bump. POP, POP, POP, POP Desmond in all black leather jacket let his 40-caliber erupted into the bartender Bmp chest. As the old man body jerked from the bullets impact as Blow kept the now lifeless old man Bumps body in front of him for protection as he held his arms tight around the dead guy's neck to hold him up. The club was clearing out quickly people screamed a broke out for the exits. Gauge heard the waring yelled to Blow from over this shoulder and quickly turned around in one swift motion. Young Patrick was only twenty-two years of age. Barely go hand on his balls yet. As he made a mistake by not shooting first BOOM! BOOM! The newest member of the Generation family did not miss his mark. The big fella stint in prison did not' out no rust on him. Gauge we're still maintaining his financial with his favorite weapon growing up for 12 gauge shotgun young Patrick flew off his feet into the Stampede of scared she lets go out his entire chest was blowing out his back there was number longer heart and lungs there nothing simply but a large hole with gauge signature written all over it below got tired of hiding behind the dead courts as he led off shots back in two Desmond direction you want my blood muthafucka you can't have my blood flow yelled out and complete rage after seeing his most trusted friend get blasted buck I can't get a clear shot that's Miguel from behind the corner of the wall he had taken cover behind gates who now head took over onto the floor behind a silver put up his index finger to his lips for Desmond to be quiet this big man crawled to the floor and to the far right of the bar and I completely different route there were below bullets were flying from Desmond watch gauge in total curiosity then it dawned on him that he had to keep below crazy as distracted so Desmond left off a few shoot into direction making blow think that day is engaged both were still hiding from his bullets boom this man heard the all to wear familiar sound and they took a quick peek all he say was Hitlers blow body falling to the ground this became out from hiding with the ear to ear smile thinking how at first he didn't trust this South Carolina cat named Gage and it didn't sit well with him when Sylvester told him that you will be on a mission in Tennessee together but it would not be with your usual partner and brother Nate but with my new investment Gauge. slowly but surely Des we are starting to like this guy he could tell by the way gauge move that the man clear did was not a rookie by a long shot Gauge stood in one spot and married his handiwork as he placed the shotgun back into his back c carrier holster, "you OK man?" Des questioned.

Yes, yes that was fun but far too easy gaze turned towards dance with the devil is grand I agree yes let us get the fuck out of here before I get a prison visit in America. Des smiled add the two men walked towards the exit and let me tell you that you don't wanna catch no present be it in the states especially in the South, 'Guage The southern exit no doubt I believe you on that", Des dapped the big fella up As I stood in the double door entrance "You we almost forgot, Sylvester said turn this bitch to ash afterwards, Des remembered. "Well shit let's not just stand her let's make it happen and set this bitch ablaze!" Word beyond bond to that." Des replied.

***

25 minutes later down the street at a local convenience store as police raced by.

"Yo Ma you did a great job at that club," Des gave his homegirl praise. Although sky was a Big Block. She was cool as hell and loyal to her long-time childhood sweetheart Desmon. Sky was Des main broad to callup. When he needed a nigga dealt with in the worst way. Sky wa his where did that and he had mad love for her. the girl came down from Toronto with Gage in him Scott loved to travel to the big girl was very sensitive about her weight, but she could play a role down to a core, thank you Des. she hugged him from outside of her waiting taxi as this broke her off proper for her services and playing below hotheaded temper against him it had worked like a charm sky being nosy at the bar and acted as if she knew two girls who had left her lonely at the bar was all acting as if she knew the two girls you better get going, Des say it as he rubs fast pregnant belly with his hand and make sure you feed my child on that flight do you know I got you she gave this a quick pic on the lips and waved bye to gauge who was sitting in the SUV waiting.

Chapter Four
Southside Philadelphia PA

Why Desmond and Gage was busy in the South taking out Robert Harris senior biggest money making club spots in Tennessee South Carolina Georgia and Florida tar baby and Olga were busy in Philadelphia airing the fuck out Robert Harris singer had stashed spots all kinds of illegal activities running out of salons and clothing stores the man had informants on payroll and police as well he had eyes and ears all over the East Coast it was 8:30 AM as the heart and soul hair salon was running business as usual on this particular Thursday morning Corey and Linda was there only two workers at the shop Korean Linda was only at the salon so early because of their regular customers couldn't make it at 10:00 AM opening time koi was a 29 year old homosexual he was light screening and had a slim build Needless to say he was all boned he kept on mini Afro all the time now his cousin Linda was appetite woman at age 26 she never had any complaints about her body for men she was a thick brown skinned sister with almonds shaped eyes her long black hair was down to the center of her back so she kept her hair in cornrows on the regular," miss Beverly how do you want this mess done today Cora ask with the smile baby I don't give a damn I know it's a hot mess that is why I came to Korea the best miss Beverly is high 5 Corey as he's run her around in the Barber chair and began to comb his favorite customers dry scalp yeah girl who took out your braids and didn't even watch this Bush clear teased honey shut your mouth that is why I pay you the big bucks every two weeks Beverly stated but I can't argue that Corey snapped his fingers miss Beverly be breaking you off properly Linda invaded the conversation Linda was smiling to herself and setting up her small hair station when Dominique and her two little girls into the shop Dominic how I like my little girls Linda asked and both sources Rana gave Linda big hug both girls were a year apart one was eight and one was nine the little girls favorite their mother Dominic was Dominican and still had a banging body girl I hate' cause it's snowing so hard out there other than that both your angels would be in school not at home nagging me all day Dominic complained well let me use the bathroom and I'll be out to attend you guys Linda said as she handed off and took the back to handle her business everyone's attention was caught off guard when the bell rang above in front door began to ring together then came a white one with the windbreaker on I'm always dressed from head to toe in white everything even her snow boots were all white with little cream color fur at the top of sticking out. She did not speak or anything and she swayed her hips from side to side the two little girls hold onto their mother Dominique but some strange reason they were afraid of the stranger hello ma'am how may I help you Corey asks as he momentarily stopped soaping up miss Beverly scalp, from the looks Corey could tell she was an American. Hello we would like a relax a kid and my nails done please they're trying to say it asks she hopped up in the spin around chair at Linda her station, "child are you something," Corey said we don't do damn nails in here The stranger we climbed back in the chair in North Korea's comment in the latter of miss Beverly all together as a strange woman leaned back her hoodie fell out for her head revealing she had a clean shaved head but she ain't even got no hair crazy damn woman edit dash at wrote in laughter at the carries crazy comment the two little girls held their hands up to their ears because that is what their mother told them to do whenever wrong folks started cursing up in the shop the stranger gave us energy green as she turned towards quarry that last comment by Cory made the woman gave him a look it look he would never ever forget I got your btich right here flag the strange woman said as she swung her chair around with her right foot and withdrew her AK47 that she could sealed somewhere inside of her big windbreaker coronary salad coming as a bullet found is marked pending Corey up against his station window behind him almost builder could do was scream as her mouth was now left wide open as her body jerk bounded in the small spin chair she sat in all the bullets ripped through her chest as a bullets rang out spraying Dominic in her two little girls ran towards the exit but from all the screaming that the little girls were doing they never even heard when their mother dropped behind them as bullets from the AK hit Dominic in the back she was there before she even hit the ground the two little girls started busting through the interest as they both of them was met with a guy whom they saw earlier shelter snow in front of the salon the girls row stood frozen in time as a dark skinned man let out two sides from the 38 Special to the girls heads the man didn't even blink I think he was trained killer and didn't show no more mercy no remorse this was how time baby was raised up in the islands he tucked his weapon as he overstep both small bodies before his feet as he entered the heart and soul hair salon ogre had Linda held at gunpoint hands raised above her head who do we have here my lady talk baby acts in a heavy accent oh just one of the hiding in the bathroom OK say it she says that the stat is in the back office in the desk lower Olga stated proudly please don't kill me I want to tell anyone I swear Linda said through sobs FCK with her talking it better be there talk baby greeted his gold teeth together moments later he returned with two trash bags filled up all of this bitch tried to hold out I found money in the rooftop also yeah stupid btich boom all the blue Linda head clean off as tar baby and her made the exit.

Buffalo, New York

Boss generation has strong first blood sentence of Elsa has hit us all around broad from the South to the north all the East Coast we have lots of money through our salons and nightclubs they have now killed your Tennessee Lieutenant below yes young nephew Corey as well Cannon report it. as he now took his seat in his right-hand chair next to his boss Robert Harold, senior "thank you" Canon.

Robert said Eddie start his feet and walked over to the window that overlooked the entire city his meeting only consisted of his right hand man cannon and his two most trusted lieutenants Bruce and ray whom Robert had working under him since day one Bruce and ray went to high school with Robert Harrell singer back in the day the three has always been close friends young Robert Harrison was considered self in high school everyone felt he only hid behind his father's reputation and organized crime family one day after getting a pass from his fourth period teacher Mr. Banks Robert left out of class for restroom break once he walked into the restroom there was three bullies guys who was skipping class and shooting dice the crew rated until Robert came out of the stall from taking the piss but out of nowhere Bruce and blitzed Robert Harold the bullies were having their way with him as he laid on the cold bathroom floor curled into a fatal fetal position. As three kids stopped away and begin to take off Roberts fresh Jordans I don't know where Bruce and Trey even the odds out entering the restroom as Dre who was always a fat kid hit one guy with a fist that knocked the poor boy out cold Bruce was a Smith one of the two who always carried around a box cutter Bruce likes a little the bullet across the face bloodshot out onto Bruce shirt from the fresh open wound the young bullet fell down to the floor crying the third kid got like and ran as fast as he could by the time the third kid came back from a school security guard there laid his two bullet friends straight shooters one was still knocked out cold the other was in the nice open wound on his face with sobbing to himself as he face the corner pull bold was in time out and he was straight in state of shock from the events that taking place what happened young man and why are you facing that corner the spirit of God staff asks the boy was scared shiftless as he could barely speak through sobs as he the woman was on his face fuck blood I'm not supposed to move without shoes the boy repeatedly spoken this out loud the child had under Go counseling from that day forward Needless to say he never told the bully never took anyone shoes ever again and since that day Robert at his new friend is Bruce and ray were inseparable.

"Attention gentlemen be on point at all times I have a lot of plans already in the works and not to mention that ace in the hole that will surely bring down the Canadian cartel we will not panic at all my friends" Robert Harold stated as he turned back around from the window to face his most trusted guys of his Harold mafia rubber hell studied the eyes of three men he trusted with his life pleased that he saw no weakness nor fear in their eyes so he turned around with the speech, "Now listen very closely gentlemen it is very true that our past month we have taken last it's nothing that we cannot overcome or bounce back from."

"Excuse me boss." Bruce stood to his feet interrupting his longtime friend speech had Robert hair I drew down heatedly in admiration he did because he hated to be interrupted and admiration because he and Bruce go so far back, and Bruce never bit his tongue he spoke his mind and always had balls. "You're excused, Bruce you may proceed." Robert Harold had said bitterly. Thank you Sir but I believe I speak for all of us when I say we want to now shed their blood and eye for an eye a 242 Bruce finished taking his seat my friend I understand and I love your loyalty to this family and yes you will get your wish I intelligence has informed me that Sylvester has his daughter Sonia going to college here in the United states Robert gave a wink smile what steak Sir Dragas curiously Virginia my friend and this is where you improves coming in I want you guys to handle that for me Sylvester would never leave her alone when we are in the middle of a war so take heed to every word sign would be under someone's watchful eye Bruce and Dre nodded their heads in unison with bright definitely smiles my family this war is ours generation believes their walls are impenetrable. and I got it right in the apple or should I say ace in the hole right inside of their family ready to take them down on my command so let's just trying to bring us down through our pockets while our ammo would bring him down through his heart I will take away all of his children and then his wife surely will go insane Robert gave us into smart Sylvester's balls are in the palm with my hand and it's time to squeeze let's go gentlemen applied pressure from all angles I am a monster and I refuse to let our family surrender understood Robert asks yes Sir everyone yelled.

Chapter Five
Toronto Ontario 7:36 am

Chung was a young beautiful woman she had been working as a only made other generation family household for now over seven years it was investor who had given her the opportunity to better herself as one day iceberg was driving came back from out of town meeting the two men was riding through Chinatown in Toronto ON, Canada as experts landed on the brakes when a young teenage girl appeared out of nowhere the young Chinese was crossing the street with her head down not even paying attention the Rolls Royce was inches away from ending her young life iceberg with the little horn for the rage cursing young girl out of her name Sylvester took complete notice of the situation he lowered his tenant window and called out to the young Chinese girl the girl was hesitating at first because she did not want to expect from three strangers" don't be afraid of me I just want to have a word with you Sylvester say it calmly after telling iceberg to calm down and let him handle the situation the young Chinese girl walked to the window slowly she was sitting a bit shaky up from being almost hit by the Rolls Royce limousine what is your name young lady Sylvester ask Key Chun, Sir I'm sorry about she was momentarily cut off by Iceberg once again outburst. "You are damn right you sorry you could have gotten me in my boss killed." he screamed at anger before iceberg continued, he caught the cold stare that Sylvester was given him and quickly shut his mouth. Key Chung how old are you?" so there is a question." "I'll be 18 tomorrow Sir" she answered with a light smile so fast I had a heart for those less fortunate living in the streets he always believed in giving folks the opportunity to better themselves and their current situation Sylvester noted that the young lady had on dirty clothes. Key Chug head holes in her jeans and her dingy shirt hung off her shoulders obviously it was too large for her to wear her hair was in a dried up on her tail so that's the skin in her arms and saw no trace of Key Chug The use of drugs he couldn't tell what she been through but it new the young lady before him was living a rough life Key Chung caught so versus eyes roaming her body and sheet it stop so that's it took notice and quickly dismissed her thoughts . "Key Chung, I'm not a pervert nor a pimp you don't have to be afraid or ashamed besides I have a daughter near your age," so there's a good tale that his statement gave her some relief but deep down she knew he was ready to do as he's say because she would never allow her mother and baby sister to go hungry where is your family young lady my father left shortly after my baby sister was born and my mother does her best to provide for my sister and I we live in that building over there ketone pointed in direction she was headed rundown apartment building.

so that was familiar with the building's daily activities and drugging and horn going all throughout that place so that's a little how the young lady was well mannered how long have you been selling your body for Johns so that's the X bold iceberg hustling their entire conversation young Kee Chung dad is trying to suspicious this one how he knew such a thing because she never mentioned it and she was now contemplating on running because this man could be the police so that's always had the ability to read people well it has always been one of his great strengths he noticed her look of shock," do you think I did not know sweetheart I'm Sylvester Maccin know everything in my sitting he stated. upon the mention of his name the young lady players are bright smile" you're the man that they all call God," she asks so that's a chuckle to himself because he too has heard people called him that before "yes Key Chung, some will say that" "now please answer my question sweetheart he said flatly," "since I was 16 years of age she answers as she heard here down in shame and began to sew up a little from the conversation she just confessed because she never told her mother nor her sister what she did to bring home money every day

so better reached out and placed a hand over the shoulder" don't cry sweetheart be strong for your family because those days of your past are over so faster say it in a serious tone," Key Chung looked up with a tear stained face curious as to what the hell he was talking about "go tell your mother that struggles are over that you now work for me and my wife." "Really," Key Chung and for the huge smile. "I don't lie nor make empty promises you don't have to pack a thing my wife will make sure you have all your needs." OK Mr. Sylvester Sr she says it there is one thing, Key Chung," "anything Mr. Sylvester." "He said with a raised eyebrow out of curiosity you can see if I'm money to your family, but they will never visit you and you will go see them on holidays because of the life I live these are the rules Sylvester said seriously.

After that day Key Chung was little to Sylvester in his generation family forevermore Herman over her head never wanted for nothing never again, she's mouthing herself as she drove past the apartment building she once lived it was a sunny day as she maneuver the Gray Maybach limousine in and out a backup traffic she shouted to the back of the limousine where are we headed to MMs Maccin? Key Chung asked. "Our destination is the union bus station downtown not too far from the Sky dome, Ajah Maccin the first lady of the Canadian Cartel said. "Mrs. Maccin, I love you as if you where my own mother's offense is going to pitch a fit when he finds out that we left this state without his permission and without supervision," Key Chung said nervously. "Key Chung Id I understand that you are Sylvester sweetheart, and he cares for you as a daughter, but I can manage my husband I take full responsibility of this you would not be the one to blame I appreciate your loyalty and concerns for our safety," Ajah said.

"Yes Ms. Maccin , I do not wish to be upset all the father figure I've ever had.", Key Chung say why diverted her gaze from the rear view window she didn't want Ajah Maccin to notice the guilt behind their eyes because deep down she had suppressed feelings for pastor but idea was well aware of Key Chung wanted her husband for herself she had never questioned key child northwester but she made a mental note to investigate key child bedroom the first chance she got.

The two women waited patient in front of the union station as the bus from Buffalo New Your pulled into the station. Ajah was strapped at all times. Just as her husband had trained her to be. She uncurled her seat belt and removed the small baby nine gun from out of her purse. She made sure it was loaded and ready to go. As she tucked her weapon in the small of her back in her tight jeans. She knew that her ass crack would not let the weapon move from out of place. It is another reason she wore no panties on this day and hardly never did at all. As she exited the Maybach limo. "Key Chung stays on point. you know we are at war leave nothing to chance anything look suspect. Pop off an ask question later. "Key Chung smiled as she gripped her own baby nine laced on her. "Are you strapped?" she questions the first lady in her best of English, "Sweetheart do not as questions that you know the answer too.: with every step Ajah Maccin knew she was still all dat! She knew that Key Chung was jealous and intrigued by her beauty. So, she purposely put on a show. For the hater she left in the car who wanted to be like her.

Chinese girl anything and hated her at the same time I can mixing would always make slip marks like sweetheart this or that because it was the name Sylvester gave Keith Chung from day number one idiot bitch she twenty-five and do not have a single curve to her body and think she wanna be me. that flat television body please Ajah thought to herself as she walked into the union bus station with a pimp in every step let it onlookers know that she is that bitch!

They say Lee trash in the garbage Key Chung said out loud and she's trying to figure out why Sylvester love that piece of trash that just walked and to Union Station she had already you're playing at low if she allowed the words from Rihanna and Drake what's my name song he charm began to unbutton her seven jeans is holding her heralded shape but she preyed on one in the public parking lot could see what she was doing in the tent it may back she was always having hot flashes and wet dreams over Sylvester Mccinn. She wanted the elder man in the worst way although she would never admit it out openly crown was obsessed with the generation files right now her juices were flowing like crazy, and she began to finger herself and moan aloud she knew she was making a mess underneath herself, but ketone did not give him lying flip opposite was simply on fire and she had only a craving for Sylvester's

just as she was coming up on comics she noticed that idea was coming out of the Union Station carrying a book bag over her shoulder with a smile that she tongue never saw before as she lowered the window just a little to air out the limo of her juices smell that at invaded the car she saw that I did was not alone she was walking with a guy who keep trying new she thing before but she couldn't figure it out until the guy and Andrew got closer interview it then hit her like a building crashing down onto her head Smurf the only child that the Maccin had home she never got a chance to meet he was in a lot of pictures and artist and services bedroom keep trying remembered the other day she was cleaning their bedroom and wondered when would he be home now her question was answered Smurf resembled his mother more than his father Sylvester, key Chung remember never ever spoke good about him he just say he serving time down in South Carolina keep trying put a fake smile as mother son entered the car

Chapter Six
Pawleys Island, South Carolina
Abandon Warehouse Meeting-Parkerville Rd

"Gentleman it is nice of you all to have made it on such short notice my friends and enemies alike." Don Anderson said as he continues to scan the small group go of Elite guys in attendance everyone in the building was about making money one way or another. "There this meeting is strictly for all the bosses as you can see there are no fill in representative in the building today, we have Mooja a little in the Islam nation. he is a brother who wants peace and works in Salem North Carolina for the children many families there who are also Muslim we have to my far right Robert Harrell senior who proudly represent the herald mafia family here to voice his opinion on the war at hand that has going on with him and Sylvester and the Canadian cartel." he paused briefly "Front and center of me is no other than Alger the dawn of soul leader of the Texas cartel he won't answer to the loss of money that his family is undergoing and the last but not least I am your host Don Anderson and leader of Florida mafia family. let me know if you like to speak first but I thank you for your generosity, but I will take this one done Anderson sneered. "now you may wonder why I did not state my business here this evening or why I called for such a meeting at short notice I will answer that shortly my friends and enemies alike I know we all can sense in the building hanging over us like a cloud of smoke it was very thick no question a lot of us despise the other and share strong dislikes for one another and rightfully so people but this is about balance today This is why I ask all of you to leave your men and weapons outside the building Texas down elder stood to his feet no offense but I am very busy man save time is meant money now why isn't Sylvester here good question because I didn't invite him Don Anderson raised his voice obviously annoyed for the interruption now Robert you is Sylvester is causing us our problems in our Rapid City in areas a lot of us has invested in your family and now slowly but surely your money is coming up short Don Anderson say it as he took his seat in the center of the small circle and I'd Robert Harrell senior so did everyone else in the room Robert still to speak after adjusting his necktie he hated to explain himself too anyone let alone these guys but he did so understood why I should be upset, "thank you, Don I understand for the floor and scheduling this meeting my friend Sylvester is a greedy knucklehead as you Roberts said with a smirk the entire group shared a small chuckle together because everyone knew it was a very true understatement he wishes to take over the entire East Coast from top to bottom he's playing is not to harm your territory but he wants to take over by areas that my brothers I will not allow Robert Harris senior add everyone surrounding him being sure he was clear that he was in a person or the weak link now I have tried to diffuse the situation but it was of no use blood is being shed as we speak the war has already began.

Muslim, Manji stir to his feet, "excuse me Robert but I am aware of the beef and longtime rival between you and two families so that's it is indeed out of control and I am not sure of his intentions if he was a take over my entire city hill furthermore the state of North Carolina I shall back you up and the entire Harold mafia family 100%," Muslim said as he sat back down. "Thank you, manager my family and I are grateful for, the very loyal and trust in us Harold mafia shall have your back as well" Robert.

the toolbar men stood quickly again." no problem I am blowing to you to assure the safety of women and children in the hoods of the state but I want to make it clear I trust not you only Allah," he scanned the room once more and said to the other parties as well I trust all the allowed as he took his seat again.

Texas stated, "I have been you connect for years the only Caucasian man said but I am no fool Robert or single it's ridiculous to believe you can beat Sylvester and the generation Canadian cartel I would not support the insane war I am pulling out no hard feelings, but I will not lose money Robert," Texas took his seat. Robert head singing not his head and said understood but before Robert Harris senior could speak again that Don Anderson stood up to speak, "Fuck all the bullshit the mid-20s African American man said you would suggest are both our constant everyone money and I refuse to let you all take food out of my two little girls mouth now somebody better write with church. "Florida mafia is going to take it to war with you both he said "I think you both know that my family is most well connected because when I declare war, I bring the Russians the Mexican cartel with me Don Anderson said given his word time to sink into everyone's mind. Making sure that I understand it the Florida mafia will steal most strongest in the powerful now Robert you need to hurry up and finish this award before I have to step in and save everybody money not enter to set back down Robert Harris singer was sweating bricks he was angry because he hated the Reds and he didn't allow anyone speak down or him like Don Anderson just did he swallowed his pride and tongue because he knew he did not want a problem with the Florida mafia fellas how are end the meeting on this note I will deliver the killer below to Sylvester sooner than later my intelligence has informed me that my secret weapon has made it into the enemy line I will be victorious and continue to hold my crown Don Alger I respect your opinion and mania thank you for your support without acknowledging Don Anderson Robert herald senior said I will win make no mistake about it how mafia fear no one nor back down from anyone through gritted teeth Robert Holsinger mean mugged on Anderson the Florida mafia leader was unmoved and unfazed as he smiled.

Virginia

"Damn!", I can't believe his mom we believe it knyga you're going to be a father so you see you smiling in the ear she had just broken the news tonight who was extremely excited the couple was headed to Toronto there wasn't out of Virginia yet sung you had just left campus for the final time until the war had subsided the doctor told her the great news just earlier that day before class. "So, what are we going to name my son?" Nate ask why driving the SUV. but who says we having a boy the devil is a liar she said still cheesing well I like nick junior mom signing watched him upside his head OK if it's a girl we'll name her name Nitesh"? she said laughing sunburst I laughing into how stupid her love was her train of thought was broken as she saw her daddy number flash up on her cell screen Sony place word finger up hold on baby it's my dad she said hello dad no Sir he's right here with me put it on speaker lake said song did as she was told daddy yeah Princess I'm here boss she wanted to speak with me Nate took over the conversation how long before you and my daughter arrive in Canada Sylvester quizzed unsure Sir I'll say sometime tomorrow morning Nate replied good because I would like you to meet my youngest son Smurf and also signing needs to reunite with her brothers OK boss I got you and Nate yes Sir balls don't do anything stupid with my Princess and if you get sleepy pulled that damn car over and my clear Sylvester questioned in a seriousness yes Sir like say it in a little town as he glanced over at Sonia who was shaking her head side to side telling that no don't tell dad that she's with child Nate read his woman through her eyes late felt some type of way but he bit his tongue as he listened to Sonya speak with her mother Roger and Smurf also before she hung up. they wrote a size for about 3 minutes after shining ended the call she loved late too much and let him remain angry she knew how to well he wanted her to tell her family especially her father Sylvester baby look once we get to this state I promise you that we will break the news to everyone OK she said sighing leaned over and plays both her hands two frame legs face and turned him her way for a quick kiss Nate pulled away what are you trying to make me read more he says smiling no never that but I got you smiling you know why I'm going to tell my family you know how much I love you and know about the baby we're expecting Nate said add suddenly he yelled oh shit as he slammed on brakes but it was too little too late they collided into the back of a suburban that was right in front of them on the Interstate the windshield exploded shattered glass back into the faces of cyanate Nate clutched onto his chest and extensive pain or the impact of the crash his chest collided with this turning wheel knocking the air out of him momentarily Nate looked over into songs direction and notice that her love mother his child was out cold blood poured out down from her temple sign had a small pieces of glass stuck into her face just like Nate had in his Nate as became watery as he silently cried to himself that she wasn't dead baby wake up don't die on me he said as he maneuvered himself over to sign in place two fingers with her neck to check for a pulse next side deeply as he was relieved that Sonia was only unconscious don't worry baby I'm gonna handle this Nate said likely trap as they exit the up truck his body was aching all over the early morning traffic was slow only a few 18 Wheelers were passing by looking at the wreckage no one bothered to stop and help next numbered over two all-white suburban truck get lockout that truck you stupid fuck." he shouted as he withdrew his Glock what if I haven't took a with the driver side of the complete frustration before Nate could get a good look into the tinted truck. BOOM! BOOM! Was our night heard as the black wanted to the suburban shattered and the desert eagle rounds found its mark into the chest of Nate which sent Nate flying backwards off of his feet blood pulled out the side of next month as he laid down on the pavement all he could muster out of his mouth were light grunts as he watched the large men exit the back of the suburban they eyes barely open darted around for his weapon but he knew in all honesty that he couldn't get to it fast enough he tried realization hit home as he knew it was set up the suburban on purposely slammed on his brakes. Dre jump his large frame into the passenger seat at the suburban truck hurry the fuck up Dre barked venomously has now Nate steel lined in the same position watched the helplessly as Bruce ran up to the SUV intently rolled the hand with eight under the SV truck with rapid speed Bruce took off running he hopped into the driver seat at the all-white suburban and speed away into now all coming traffic other Interstate late heard horns blowing from afar but all he could do was nothing he was similar conscious and helpless used it to the love of his life tears rolled down the corner of Nate size in a matter of seconds the SUV exploded right before an 8 he was just a distance away as he could feel the breeze in the breeze from the explosion next closed his eyes and prayed to die as the last thing he saw was a huge fireball left into the sky in the dark sky hovering over the death of his soul mate and unborn child.

Maccin Estate

The pool hall located in the South wing the Maccin state was rocking as it was a clue tar baby lyrics back in his seat and I had the scene before him he smiled to himself and married his handiwork it was a family affair to say the least," you didn't have to throw me at home coming party Tar," Smurf said while struggling to keep that Jamaican weed smoke in his lungs. "Nah man, you have always been my little family. Even back before you ever knew what pussy taste like, "Tar said smiling. Tarbaby was high as a fool, fool. It was natural to him. He got high all day every day. It was in his nature. He had been a part of the Maccin family fare well over 13yrs. Tar always proved on consistent basis. That his loyalty lies with the Generation. Before any and everything Sylvester has always been like a father to him. Just as much as he was a father figure to everyone else. Even to this day at age twenty-seven. Tarbaby still considered Smurf father his mentor and father. Although prison time had change Smurf just a little, he now had a few tattoos and a clean-shaven head. To Tar he was still the little teenager who use to follow him around." so, you going to stay your *** out of trouble or what Smurf?" Olga asked and she took a long hard drive from the blood and continued to rotation that our baby next in line as the three of them took shot after shot of eight of spades drink standing to his feet while having little, "I'm good, Olga don't sweat the fires baby," Smurf slurred. "OK badass, whatever you say." Olga said with a wave overhanging not convince or believing anything Smurf was saying. smart felt a hand on his shoulder incarcerated no elder friend the familiar voice to Smurf said as he turned around to a smiling Gauge. the two men DAP up and embrace one another in abruptly hood the two cellmates had not seen one another since the day Sylvester free gauge from prison Smith would never forget the day that gave saved his life from the South Carolina cribs he stood back from Gage and looked the huge man in the eyes thank you for saving my life Smurf say it in a broken tone. "Bro, what I tell you about thanking me I did what I was supposed to do besides, Pam I should be thanking you for introducing me to your father." Greg said in a Husky voice." well man I guess you two are even." type ABC it why under two men before him through hazy vision gauges for both smiled and nodded their head in agreement Gauge felt the magnetic eyes of the Russian beauty bombshell all him he instantly looked in her direction she add him seductively hello gate he took all of grin from her lip gloss full lips and short skirt to her voluptuous body in perfectionist tone legs. "Wuz up ma?" "You" she answered quickly. Gauge smirked at her boldness flirtation. "Here we go with love shit man," Tar said in his heavy accent. Olga shot Tar the bird finger and blushed. "Yo you two know it's true." Smurf said smiling because he could send the attraction between hit too. Gauge grabbed the back of Smurf neck playfully. "Mind grown folks business boo." He said in the southern accent. Smurf place both hands in the air as to surrender. "Care to join me for a walk?" Gauge asked Olga while extending his hand for her to grab hold of. "Certainly." She said with a little schoolchild grin. And you still do her feet out of her chair in her all-blue fuck me pumps. she grappled gauge hand, and he led the way hey man I do not know about you but these two do not blow my hair with all that love bullshit Tarbaby smashed the small lit roach out in the ashtray. "Excuse us for a second thought damn said in our series song no problem, man tar said as he stood to his feet while from himself so now you are ghosts coming from out of nowhere and shit Smurf slurred you would have noticed me if you had been on point." Damon said in a bitter tone. Tension was thick between Sylvester only two sons. "You fuck you bro.!." do you have a statue were better than me Mr. daddy's favorite Smurf said sarcastically I'm not the blame for your gambling and drug problem things were well when you was gone I will not let you destroy our family Damon was now face to face with his younger brother he could now smell the alcohol on Smurf breath Smurfs the hood sadly in tears and heartbroken if you are the cause of one single tear to mom's eyes I'll kill you myself Damon said sternly.

Chapter Seven
A local Virginia Hospital

The Mercedes-Benz came to a screeching halt in front of the crowded hospital there is no wasted no time at all jumped out of the car and ran towards the entranceway leaving sky is sitting duck he had absolutely no intention on waiting on her big pregnant ass when his brother needed him the most. Desmon emerged from the revolving door and ran straight up to the receptionist desk .the young Asian girl never looked up from playing a game on the computer could feel every bit of the wind of Desmond the man was literally moving that fast, "where is my brother who was rusted moments ago?" this act out of breath the agent girl never looked up from playing a game on a computer until Desmond pounded his face hard on the counter top. "BITCH!," I know you hear me he yelled. the reception Asian family looked up now paralyzed in fear as she looked at the small necklace that read generation on her chain, she was familiar with the cartel the agent woman caught deuces real quick like because she didn't want to end up fighting or floating off the shore of Virginia Beach the crime family generation was notorious even down in the southern part of the United states. "I'm sorry Sir what is his name?" the reception asked it's Nathan Washington Sky answered as she came up and stood beside the father of her child sky knew that dance wasn't in the mood for bullshit she had walked up just in the time to save the young Asian girls behind the desk, Des calm down baby names going to make it she said as she wrapped her arm around his waist he was going through the motions as he just stared a murder hole through the receptionist girl.

Des, remain silent as he thought of what his baby mother sky just said he's going to make it but there's had to be sure besides the baby that sky was carrying Nate was the only family by bloodline that he had left that was young and his only brother the two of them been through it all together this man drifted back to the call he had gotten not even 30 minutes ago is this Mr. Washington the caller asked yes it is who is this this asks this is detective Lewis Miller I have your brother cell phone I was calling to inform you that there has been an accident concerning Nathan my office and I found it cell phone in the pocket and strolled the call log for a family member to speak with and I came across here in man that your name that said brother beside it.

Desmon felt like he couldn't breathe as a detective updated him on the harbor if events that had taken place on that Interstate this was just in the process of packing his shit to head back up to Canada since he knew Nate and Sonia chose to take the highway instead of flying he and Scott were just about to head to the airport so they could catch their flight back north the couple was already ready to check out of their four season hotel. "Sir, Mr. Washington is in room 123, but we will he be heading back into surgery shortly the aging girl stated with rapid speed dead's and sky were off hand in hand in route the room 123, Des needed to know his baby brother status he needed reassurance that Nate would be all right this guy made it way to room 123 without knocking to the entered the room. Nate laid there motionless in the hospital bed he had Two's running from out of his arms and he had some stuck up his nose his head was heavily wrapped although the young gangster eyes were closed you could still tell that he was a lot of pain from the look of his face sky quickly covered her mouth with her hand and shook her head back and forth in total disbelief there was a doctor stated over young late checking his vital signs may I help you the doctor asked yes Sir I'm Desmond Washington his brother then stated his voice cracking down from the side of his brother fucked up this way the old white man turned around and extended the hand for a firm handshake there's acknowledging and shook the doctors hand we have been expecting you Sir the detective told me he called you doctor said my name is doctor fellows your brother is a strong one and also may I say a lucky one doctor fellers remove his glasses from his face and pocket them lucky they said you say he was shot twice to the chest error and one bullet did damage to his lungs but that bullet went out through the back the other bullet barely missed his heart but that one is stuck in the back around shoulder blade area my staff and I will be removing that bullet shortly liar brother did suffer some head trauma from hitting that concrete after he was shot but certainly All in all he should have good recovery Dr fellow said with a smile of confidence this feels just a little bit better knowing his brother would pull through but he still felt some kind of way because he knew that the Harold mafia was behind this bullshit this fight tears away and concealed his emotions he wanted to make the herald mafia pain in the worst way's death heart was frustrated and it wouldn't heal until he got his revenge back did you two know the young lady that Mr. Washington was within that terrible bombing SUV tragedy Dr fellow quiz Sky lips quivered as she was about to say yes but Desmond cut her off no Sir we did not know her he said as he gave sky cold hard stare that spoke volumes well what a shame poor girl never stood a chance police said they could barely tell that it was a woman, doctor said shaking his head. be back in a few to get your brother doctor fellows made his exit from the room.

"Yo Sky I know what you're thinking but we can't trust that doctor that's why I said no we did not know Sonia because there will be all our investigation behind this," Des said. "I understand baby," Sky said as she walked over and touched it young legs hand," "damn I hate to be the bearer of bad news, but I must call Ajah and Sylvester," Des said as he took out his cell.

Back in Toronto Canada

It was like a fifteen round heavyweight title match to see who would tap out first as gauge and all the literary tour the small motel room being apart now the two of them were on the floor enjoying their sexual exploitation it was not like Mr. and Mrs. Smith up in the kitchen, but it was damn near close enough. "OH, Shit Baby," yes that's it Fuck me Hard." Olga shouted. as he laid flat out on her back gauge continued to power her with three strokes her legs were up on his massive shoulders as sweat drops fall from off of gauges face he loved to look into her irresistible eyes the two have been going at it for well over an hour, 'FUCK baby you about to make I make a bus again." gays roared not yet not yet toggle smiled seductively lay down on your back she requested out of breath anyway gays did as Olga asks the center of her slippers just wear on the air and he didn't know that Russian let it could be so good Olga was full of energy and confidence before he knew it his tests were in her mouth as she sucked on both of his nuts at the same time by squeezing his round manhood with her left hand gauge was losing his mind as he moan and groan he took his time to enjoy the view before him , you trying to punishing a brother ma." Turning on the top of Gauge all gave him my view of her plump round as it jiggle like jello with her back towards him she squatted down and hovered over the top of Gauge semi long hard penis taking his length in inch by inch he watched on amazement as she eased down on top of his erect penis his manhood with both of her hands Gage was losing his mind as he moaned and groaned once again Olga stopped. NAH, NAH, NAH you about to cum yet. she gave a devilish smirk our guys could do was stare at her in total disbelief she picked up her own panties off the floor and placed them in to gauge mouth he opened wide with a smile as he could now taste her pussy juices you ready she asked he remove the painters from Miceli to answer here yeah mom send it over the top of gauge over gave him a view of her plump brown ask as it jiggle like jello with her back towards him she squatted down and hovered over the type of Gauge's hard dick. taking this length inch by inch he watched in amazement yes she eats down on top of his erect penis his manhood easily disappeared into her clean shaved pussy once she felt comfortable she began to buck on his heart on bouncing her nice ass riding reverse cowboy style position uncle was a gushy as a mother and he knew her juices were flowing out of control right that gay salad was slapping her ass .Ogle was moaning like crazy and going into a frenzy as she coated his dick with her juices Sierra climbers for the opting time she looked back her gazed over you could tell that that brought tears to her eyes you ready she acts no you ready gay said as he took her panties out of his mouth she smiled because she knew he was about to punish her now he grabbed hold of her hips and began to throw his manhood up into her guts oh over swelled his gauge pound away up into her pussy pushes take this dick Ma wanted it take this dick he demanded I am daddy fuck I am she squealed sweet voice and loans crowd pleasure was sending gauge over the edge as he picked up the pace open as was clapping as if she wore a black woman her juice began to slide down gauges testicles and seeping out of the sides in spring at lightweight the sight of this was all needed to climax. "I'm about to cum ma." He roars out loudly. "Bust in my pussy. Bust in my pussy." She moaned "Oh Fuck" he grunted as he released himself for the third time inside of her witness as I always could do was come flaps backwards onto and out of rough gauge although they had just met it felt natural for them ogre had never felt so strongly for a man from the time she first met him she knew the two of them would have something special everywhere all the ever met has been intimidated by her and her job those guys wanted to change her they didn't understand why she did what she did it was all ogre ever knew her grandfather was one of those showed her the taught her that she knew about take alive she was immune to killing and she loved the job but she now met a man that wasn't afraid of her a man who understood the life she lived a man who himself lived a similar life as well gaze kissed her fool pink soft lips as she laid on top of him trying to catch her breath So what now you gonna run back to your American girls or the question sarcastically no don't trip mom I'm enjoying my time with you and this feeling he said in a serious tone is that so she said as she add him now face to face their latest version one another as gaze created her tightly in his massive arms he looked down into her ocean blue eyes as their naked flesh generated heat against one another now you gonna have to trust me we fit well together like a glove. I'm a man not a boy I do not play games gay said with a Peck on her lips she felt the words to the heart and her eyes began to get blurry vision as she quickly diverted her gaze so he wouldn't see her emotions and laid her head on his chest she knew she could trust him and every word he spoke was true from this night falls she would hang on to his every word gauge she spoke just above a whisper what's up ma he asks never let me go she said as a lonely tears scaped her eye onto his chest no doubt baby I got you spoke confidently she wanted to kiss him again but not against it because she never wanted no man to see her emotions on display. her father was strong for hitwoman. she never shows signs of weakness, and she was not about to start instead she closed her eyes and inhaled deeply as she smiled to herself.

Buffalo New York- Robert Harold Sr. Office.

In deep thought to himself Robert Harrison was feeling himself he had just left the airport with his bodyguard and right hand man cannon Robert was skeptical about keeping his family in Buffalo NY retaliation was surely come after the death of Solomon Bruce and ray had done a wonderful job and Robert Harris senior had rewarded the two accordingly Robert wife Victoria Harold was kind and happy that was going to spend her time with her only sister in Kent WA she took the youngest two sons with her on mar 17 and next year the baby boy only 16 years old the oldest Robert Harold junior stayed behind with his father and plus he was expecting his first child with the next few days with his girlfriend Naomi so Robert junior didn't want to miss out on that you have a call Sir cannon say it as he walked into his boss office who is it Robert senior acts it's Smurf, Cannon replied.

Chapter Eight

Gauge still insert list and only a towel cover the lower half of his six one tile 245 solid frame he was now all of 36 years old a true OG to the streets of South Carolina down in the United states the big man had seen and done it all nothing his new family generation or anyone else did face him like Tupac said many things learned in prison and true indeed gauge had learned a lot in his five year stint in prison he promised himself never to allow any law enforcement to ever again take his freedom he would rather die going out blasting before he subject himself to being told what to do when to sleep when to wake up when to end your visitations and when to eat no gauge simply would hold court in the streets fires before he ever went back to hind bars again he was deep in thought as he stood on his 4th floor motel room at the window taken in the breathing site of Toronto ON city he often thought of his close friends achy lost he had found the way he felt and now it was at the explosion rating paying for headaches he woke up to no gaze had just taken a few asking for that but instead of he was beginning to feel emotions in love for a Russian queen who laid invade behind him he turned his head into her direction as flashbacks from the night before invaded his thoughts oh grand on his dick like a no woman has ever done before he smiled at the thought he watches sleep peacefully before him great examined her curves that displayed well through the covers that hugged her petite frame ogre skin was smooth like butter her short haircut only brought out her beautiful face today's Olga was perfect she understood him because she was a stone cold killer but the girl had a wonderful personality and on top of that she could relate to gauge on not having much family growing up there was only one woman that Gage cared for and she had just sent him an incoming text message. the phone vibrated engage hand as he flipped it open to read his inbox message but before he could need Reddit Olga I don't know where snatched a phone out of his hands days not South first hand while Olga was Sylvester hit woman because she was tasked to tell and very smooth because he didn't know she was awake nor did he hear or see her move on that bed it all happened so fast as if she herself was the wind yeah what the fuck is your problem Gage asks his upper lip curled into a frown and his teeth clenched together as he tried to hold back his anger he had feelings for Yum ,Yum from his old crew someone he once called sister.". Your my problem fucka." sending you're making girlfriend text message while you think I'm asleep overstated with such attitude as she flipped over the phone and checked inbox messages she was sitting straight up in the bed gave her a smirk as he didn't even trip nor made an attempt to smash the phone back the new Yum AKA Yolanda I could match her attitude who the fuck is Yolanda," Olga yelled by the tone of her voice gauge could tell that she was hurt he shrugged his shoulders and sat on the edge of the bed gave older the silent treatment as he used the remote to flip through the television channels oh you can't answer fucking you got what you wanted so it's the Russian bitch right Olga hate being ignored and she couldn't believe she trusted him and now gave just turned his back to her and watched television she noticed her vision beginning to get blurry as she saw him sent a outbox history text say he had loved and miss this girl. waiting little time overtakes who the fuck is this see that the covers off of her naked body refusing to cry she jumped up out of the bed and began to put her clothes on not giving a bath about a shower see through gaze sale at the back of his head and it landed on the bed the big men didn't budge and he didn't even entertain ogre childish ways add games watch television he thought about how Olga acted just like any other woman despite she being from the from Russia in his mood he cared for her but he didn't have time for drama and he also was not out headed to answer her questions he sat on the edge of the bed with nothing but a towel I can't believe that I thought you were different I would say as she was placing on her heels she heard the phone vibrate the weighted and anxious to see what message was coming in on the phone now she picked the phone back up from behind gauge when she read the inbox message her eyes were complete shock this is Gage sister who the fuck are you his sister Olga whispered ogre didn't reply she now saw that she made a fool of herself she stared at the back of gauge in this belief no man had ever made her feel such an idiot Olga was at a loss for words it now down on her that's why the men didn't try to stop me once I grabbed his phone buck he didn't have shit to hide ova thought to herself Olga side she walked around in to the front of the television and stood directly over gauged blocking his view of the phone but gays didn't bother to take a look at her I'm sorry baby I'm always paranoid that I've been hurt so and before she could continue gay snatches phone out of her hands without about the same rapid speed that she did to him early Ogle was too surprised at how fast the big men moved he stood to his feet until he was tired over although with his next 6-1 frame and without saying a word gaze turned away from her shaking his head as he made his way to the bathroom. "Gage I did not know that was your sister ogre shouted back the Russian beauty was still fighting back tears as he stopped dead in his tracks before entering the bathroom I gave you my muthafuckin word last night that should have been enough if you have trust issues or insecurity issues then the ships on urge not me and to clearly that stupid bitch you said earlier no I ain't got what I wanted' cause what I want is a wife not a little girl ,"gay said through gritted teeth.

as he slammed shut the bathroom door he slammed it so hard over square the room shook from the impact hits where his wife played over and over in her head she dropped her head in shame because Gage was right and all his words he just spoke were true because she did act like a little girl but what she we're still stuck on is when he said he wanted a wife Olga wasn't sure how to make it up to him but she knew she had to make this thing right she was following up with Gage already and she couldn't do anything to stop it either and she wondered what he was thinking about and what he was doing behind the bathroom door her cell phone now went off disturbing her thoughts as she rushed over towards where her phone lay on the night stand ogre looked at the screen as she saw she had her income on call from iceberg or do it had to be a good damn reason why he was calling because she is Sylvester right hand man iceberg really got along what's up Berg, Olga answered. her ears can believe what she was hearing gauge walked out of the bathroom as soon as auger dropped her phone and covered her mouth what's wrong my gaze asks as he saw the distant paper look on her face it's investor he's had a heart attack after he found out Robert herald killed Sonia I'll just say that this relief shot we gotta go mom gay say it as he hurried to put on his jeans and T shirt he's at the hospital iceberg told me I'll drive over said gays nodded his head in agreement as they couple exit the room.

Buffalo New York

"Boos you called for us," Big Dre asked. him and Bruce entered Robert Harrison's office. "Yes, Yes" Robert smiled as he motioned for abused and trade to have a seat in the two empty chairs in front of his desk Roberts sat patiently and confident behind his massive desk they had mafia landed back in the comfortable chair with his hands together over his belly he was proud of his hit me and dragon Bruce for a job executed perfectly the hit was a successful one.

Robert Harold Sr. possessed a lot of power as the head made man of his family he had become more popular than his father Monroe Harold could ever imagine his two longtime friends Bruce Andria have watched him and helped him obtain the power he now possessed today Robert was and intimidated man to all around him he sat with his trim to go T that outlined his lips he was handsome for his age the spinning waves in his head definitely made him look younger than he actually was the killer is seeking his I told the story that he was not the one to fuck with. "j job well done with my friends I knew I could always count on YouTube Robert said with a status fine grain not a problem but you know how we Rock You point them out in Bruce and I lay them down Dre spoke proudly Bruce just nodded his head in agreement he smiled at dray because as far as he could remember Dre always been a cocky arrogant muthafuckin thinking he was like Superman straight untouchable but his murder game was a one the big fella was boil like that and to say the least he was most definitely about that life hands down Bruce couldn't have wanted a better partner by his side than Dre. Robert's mountain exchanged glances with Bruce because he knew exactly what big Dre was capable of and just like Bruce, he was happy to have this insane man on his team. "listen my friends I've given Smurf the green light to handle his father for me the boy hate his old man with a passion he is truly to prove to me that he wants to be down with us but it when will he kill him because if myself do not respect what he's doing just loyalty is unacceptable in my book the boy sold out his own flesh and blood just to get down with us and free himself from prison Robert pull it out a cigar and prepared the light he took his time as he allowed his words to penetrate with his two head men Robert Harris single blew out smoke now they dig down in Florida Don Anderson feels like a fool. He was worried about losing the war to so that is a now the tide is rolling in our favor." Bruce and right listed on as they were digesting exactly everything Robert was saying Sylvester's in the hospital and will soon be that dead as a doorknob by the hands of his own son and my very own trump card one by one, we will take out Ajah and all of her Sylvester children song is already dealt with Robert said as he put out his remaining cigar.

"Sylvester wanted award now he can't handle it and I always believe when you got a man down don't let him get up to his feet generation will be grow a week my friends, we have no room for any mistakes gentlemen we were moving back to Canadian soil in a few weeks I've already made an that arrangement where I would say it with a devilish smirk, he glanced around at his two trusted men. And he could see that these two men were down with his insane idea Robert knew this would be the ultimate disrespect because he is ham family mafia was not to ever live in Kennedy again after the war back in the day his father Monroe last against Simon Maccin. his assistant cannon told him that would because suicide mission and Robert ignored his right-hand man comment deep down in sad, he knew that cannon would be down with him regardless Robert Harris senior was no fool he was definitely contemplating the possibilities of this power move, but he could care less about the level of disrespect imposed. He wanted to crush the Canadian cartel and take over the city of Toronto. "I love this idea boss disrespect Sylvester in every way possible." Dre said arrogantly I agree also Sylvester should had stopped long ago deluding himself and admitted he made a mistake for wanting a war he called not to win." Bruce said finally breaking his silence. "Glad that you all agree now get us some drinks to celebrate an early victory over generation and so you guys can help me come up with some good names for the unborn grandchild." he said. As bruising Drake shared a laugh with their balls, we bow to no one and rain in this chest game as kings Robert said puffing on another cigar.

Nearby Toronto Hospital

To say the atmosphere outside is investor magazine hospital room was fucking would definitely be an understatement everybody and their Mama was feeling the effects of the war at hanging no one knew the real status of Sylvester's health the loss of his only daughter was simply too much with the old man to handle the small hospital hallway was closed off to our visitors Sylvester Maccin im was the only one on that floor money talked bullshit walked other families and parties had to be relocated the Canadian cartel hitched me in lined the hallway heavily armed it had to be at least 30 soldiers who lined the hallway and the stairwell doctors and nurses were only allowed in the area besides members of the generation family Olga sat comfortably next to gauge who had his massive arms around her shoulders for comfort because the woman was shaking like a cold front their brains the building Olga love for Sylvester ran deep and she did not want to lose him she couldn't believe that the poor song maker was gone the poor girl couldn't even have the right proper burial Olga sugar head at the thought iceberg and tar baby still a side by side. sneering at young Smurf with hard steady eyes as Smurf felt the eyes and took another bathroom break. "Yo me yo me don't trust him man something about that kid ain't right," Tarbaby spoke in his heavy accent I am with you. As he began running his hands over his face thinking how the little man Smurf always his favorite been out of all the Sylvester children.

Young David pace to howl way in a frenzy he did his best to conceal his anger and pain he had lost his sweet sister Sonya over some mothering fuck war, but he could never blame his father for her death thoughts of her smile made tears lie down his cheeks again.

Damon always dressed hood. His hat was draped real over his designer jeans. Were baggy and two time his size. From the dip in his walk, you could tell he was investors oldest child was not one to be fucked with the boy was almost a replica of his old man he possessed that killer instinct in his eyes just like his father Sylvester there was no denying no mistake in whose son he was. his all black V neck T shirt fit over he's slim well bit frame his legs felt like pick up sticks from all the packs and back and forth but he was really too angry to feel it Damon wanted revenge in the worst way but he couldn't make a move without his father authorizing it then was also concerned about his mother Ajah see two had taken song is loud hard but his mother placed on a front end try her best to be strong for his dad deep down Damon new he also had to be strong for the family he iced out medallion swarm back and forth around his neck with each step he took the medallion regeneration similar to the one Desmond war they've been knew that there was a rat amongst the crew a sibling snake to the speak Damon didn't believe in luck there was no way that Robert Harris senior me and knew exactly where to find his sister and young Nate new Damon was smarter and sharper than a lot of people gave him credit for. He had every intention of finding who was behind his sister's death just like tar and iceberg notice Damon notice also how strangely Smurf had been acting the boy had shown no signs of emotion for his own sister loss nor did he show any concern for their very own father Damon also noted that Smurf kept disappearing for long periods of time they've made a mental note to check into it he promised himself whomever was responsible for his sister death that he will appeal their cap back.

David, I know how you feel but walking yourself to death will not change anything here come have a seat I will go say it as she scooted over so Damon could sit between her and Gauge. no I'm good then replied through gritted teeth never break your stride he continued to pace with his hands behind his back in the parade rest fashion oh shit my bad bro Smurf said nervously as he accidentally bumped into his brother Damon let's see exit the hospital bathroom Damon mean bug Smurf but gave a different smirk once he read Smurf eyes of guilt Smurf walked away clear it down Damon no know who the rat was.

Chapter Nine

Key Chung and everything went into I just draw was pulling them open one by one smelling the first lady lace panties and other clothes as well key Chung was supposed to be cleaning up their state while everyone was away at the hospital with Sylvester but instead she was snooping around the master bedroom of Ajah and Sylvester Key Chung she wanted desperate to be on your end to live the life of a first lady of an organized crime empire.

she had really gone cycle snipers' investors dress suits and underclothes the poor girl was truly sick in the head she tried different outfits of Ajah own and pretended to be the wife of Sylvester. Keith Jones are definitely add herself down in the large mirror connected to the headboard of the queen size bed he Chung didn't worry about anyone walking in on her because she knew that Audrey was not going to leave Sylvester bedside back at the hospital but what Key Chung didn't know was that iceberg and tie baby had been watching her the entire time on the monitors Key Chung sashayed around the bedroom and I just high heels and blue lace thongs. she was feeling herself as she was about to go lay down on the bed and play with herself. fabric of the thongs made her more wet but before she could she never heard nor saw him walk in ready to deal with the devil?" iceberg question as he placed his massive bear look hand over Key Chung mouth this mother her screams but there was no need because no one bullet here her if she tried. more embarrassed than afraid at the moment being caught keeps on linked back tears as she knew who now her in a fucking position had that was no doubt that the large body she felt against her back was no other than iceberg the man who never liked her from day one was Sylvester first picked her up out on the streets Key Chung always been afraid of the maniac. didn't know she couldn't run and also she knew he would tell Audrey if she didn't do as he said ketone could feel the heart on of icebergs cleaners poke her in her back she was so scared she shook under control of me I've been watching some of this Chinese push big eyes very bark as he pressed his Crouch harder up against harass now bend over bitch he demanded as he pushed keep strong forward onto the queen size bed don't do this key Chung stuttered no you wanna get the fuck by boss but he's unable to help you out so delete got you iceberg smile Key Chung didn't wanna die so she pulled her thong over to the side exposing her clean shaven pussy OK, OK she sobbed that's what I'm talking about I say it wasted no time as he inserted his stiffness into her tight wetness he Chung was so wet that iceberg worst rating in with the first throws he grunted as he reportedly pumped away. I spoke that was like the maniac he was he hit her with long deep strokes as she whimpered and cried out into the small bed pillow oh hell no bitch ice roared as he snatched the pillar and tossed it over her head I wanna hear your sex as giving her tight pussy he demanded as he picked up his pace and speed key chunk thought it was over when iceberg pulled out but the animal was far from done as he rammed his manhood into her tight pussy oh God take it out ice take it out she screaming but her request fell on deaf ears as he held her hips real steady Japanese bitch and out of her pussy all baby your ass so good I sparked out at per pleasure please come for me ice please baby come for me keep Chung spoke through Charles and she tried to urge the big fella own by no means she wasn't a rookie to get Angel action but Iceberg dick was huge and on top of that he was pumping in and out of her roughly with powerful thrusts oh excruciating pain she cried Key Chung felt pain shooting upper spine every time he went deep she was doing her best not to pass out from pain and she was trying not to lose control over her bowels over you btich Key Chung was sure that he would murk her then. yeah I'm a come for you daddy you gonna catch this hot come on your face alright he questioned as he went rapid speed in and out of her mouth yes, yes oh shit she shouted as she clutched onto the sweat of the sheets on the bed she could feel the swollen head of his penis as iceberg row it towards explosion oh shit turn around bitch he ordered Key Chung.

She barely has strength turn around as she did so and set on the edge of the bed as big iceberg releases nut all over face keep telling deepthroated his manhood to get every drop of come off no hands no hands he demanded she did her best to take all of him into her mouth without scraping her teeth on her knees porn star iceberg chuckled he would do his penis from out of her mouth key tongue fell back onto the bed her fucking ass wore out in her so the burger was simply exhausted as she laid patent against the sweated up sheets yo you straight iceberg axe he was zipping up his pants and admiring the Chinese made perky breasts that set up nicely with dark . I'm good she said unconvincingly wondering to herself why the fuck do you care but under no sticky tongue tar baby was now waiting at the door you a she's all yours babe what is that big iceberg gave the pound as he walked out we'll do more tar said as he closed the bedroom door with a satisfied smirk and last filled eyes ketone sat up on the bed and just the lace blue thongs she stole from her boss; in a baby voice is what caught her contention she saw the look in his eyes.

Chapter Ten
Somewhere In Salt Lake City

Psych hated television and radios he needed no entertainment. Soccer was a well experienced contact track killer the expiration was very good at his job no one really knew his name and no one really knew his true identity because he changed identities as much as women change shoes psycho cabin is located somewhere up in the mountains in Salt Lake City UT he was his own boss and only marched to the beat of his own drum and that was his own he wasn't a part of no cartel no army and no mafia no one visit nor did no one nowhere psycho rest is head a lot of reasons being because the guy was aggressively antisocial he was mentally ill dealing with seven mental health disorders the worst was a psychopath suffering from a mental disorder characterized by aggressive antisocial behavior to the many organizations who had hired him called him cycle for short cycle was in his mid-30s and Italian man he had a slim build frame and kept a ball headed his way his only family was his choice of many weapons that surrounded him ammunition was never a problem for psycho he had a trap door that led you down a small flight of stairs underground it was almost like a basement this is where cycle kept all his arsenal the man truly lived to kill murder for hire was the name of the game cycle has several different add salt rifles and C4 explosives he kept desert Eagles magnum pistols handguns to shotguns and even rocket launchers whatever he can't track desired he had it he could get the job done tools were never a problem for psycho he loved the snow and being alone up in the mountains despite his location he could still catch very good service on the cell phone he had just finished trying out the new night vision goggles when he helped vibration of his cell phone on his hip he unclipped his sale from the holder he flipped it open terrorist or personal, Psycho asked it was something he always asked when he answered the phone. It would tell him what kind of jobs was to be expected of him if it was personal then he knew it was just a small hit two body of man or the entire family but if the college said him terrorists, then cycle would no job was worth major cash because he would have to use explosive terrorist taxes to take down buildings and airplanes or even arenas etc. "Personal my friend," "the Harold mafia needs your assistance. Kenneth said into the phone how many heads cycle asked 3 1/2 can you say with a smile psycho sighed deeply at the task before him 3 1/2 men there was three adults and a baby involved not a problem cycle said as he wrote the information down in his little notepad". you know the drop off location and you know the price money in the briefcase and have details pictures of victims and locations for me inside a vanilla overload are we clear." psycho say it into the phone already the call had ended because he never spoke over two minute limit over the phone crystal can I replied great then contact will be complete within 48 hours immediately after this call ends and one more thing psycho I'm no one's friend psycho said venomously before he pressed the end button and ended the call.

Cannon smiled definitely as he closed shut his sale, he did not like psycho but he respected the guy for not having no friends family and anything that could ever make him weak the guy was about his business that was the Robert Harrell loved to use him and always told Kenny to call the psychopath the guys are killing machine and immune to how ever he took a life.

Sylvester's Hospital Room

Ajah Maccin laid over to kiss her sleeping husband dry lips after iceberg live the horrific news about her daughter Sonya both Sylvester and Ajah were traumatized. in a matter of seconds of Esther collapsed onto the living room floor clutching on to the right side of his chest as she why it's a vessel a motional E along tear trickled down the first lady face it starts with singing as a child disturbed her Ajah remember when Sonya was only eight years old of age she asked why is it that Bobby wasn't black, Ajah also was laying there as she hold on to her husband's hand as she cracked the smile at the thought of good memories. it relates to know the life of the kingpin in danger came with it know she was never gotten to see her only daughter again and Sylvester will never get to escort her in the church to her husband to be there will be no wedding hell they c cannot even be a burial for Sonya.

the thought of Ajah, never seen her daughter again counter to *** she had to cover her mouth and unbearable pain in her chest she thought it was a heart attack now I know my queen is not crying Sylvester asks dryly as he opened the eyes and truly to undo her cotton mouth with saliva without saying a word she hugged him the best way she could and she cried like a new born on her husband chest Sylvester rubbed his hand over the back of her back he couldn't embrace his wife like he wanted to he was still feeling the effects from all the medication the doctors had ham on he had loved her with all his soul what are we going to do are happy that your soul mate was finally awake." Damon will lead the family to victory, and I trust you to be by his side. we will win the war in avenge song is dead, "Sylvester spoke. just above a whisper. Ajah loved her man's heart and how he always had the answer to everything his pride was too strong to be broken hey all Sylvester went even being let alone be broken the leader of the Canadian cartel would not accept defeat even laying in the hospital bed after a heart attack he oozed confidence.

So, there is a dropped silent tear from the corner of his eyes as he continued to speak," I love you, but you got to be strong now." I know you have learned a lot I am being married to me he questioned with a smile I did not even hear up and down in agreement with him she wiped her eyes, and then did he is it is well your right baby it is just so damn hard when you're not in control she kissed his lips again.

trust me I understand he began to cough a lot of babies I just panicked I am good just pass me that cup with a straw in it he add the cup on the tray holder she did as he asked as he took a few sips of the water to get his vocals right he wanted had he been too aggressive or two greeted a step to Harold mafia toes. Sylvester could see the restless rings around her eyes plus her eyes were puffy and red get some rest from me OK but baby you were all she got out of her mouth before Sylvester shook his head let her know his save was final and not to be challenged. Ajah knew he was right and she also knew not to ever challenge her man's decision the only time she would really argue for anything was when it bold Smurf although she would never hurt Smurf was her favorite out of all three because she always knew he was a troubled child and needed special attention that only a mark a mother could give that was the only time that was persistent in getting her way so that's a new that while he laid on his back trying to recover his end resort applying pressure from all angles and right now he needed his wife to listen in obey what he said he didn't need her against him but it's dead with him he had loved his only daughter to death and his wife knew this as well but there was no time to mourn her death and his wife knew this as well but there was revenge simply no room to be weak or they would surely die. I just heard the door in the room open she looked over to see the small African American nurse into the smiles oh you're up she asked surprised yes finally add you answered sarcastically for him the nurse checked his post you needed a lot of calories for your heart Mr. McGee I'm OK he said unconvincingly stop being hard headed I just say it with a smile no you will be OK after regaining your strength nurses here at him algebra paired to leave I'll be back in the morning please listen to the hospital staff I should clear with him yeah alright he answered aggravated Sylvester hated being told what to do but he knew his wife and the nurse were right I'll be checking on you periodically through the night the nurse said with the friendly smile as she began to head out of the room.

Chapter Eleven
Maccin Estate, Toronto Ontario

As soon as Ajah Maccin and got back to the states she was looking to go get some rest I bought it was feeling effects of no sleep in several days she craved a hot shower and a chance to sleep tough to be in her own sheets but before she could get up the wrap around stairs middle of the living room floor I've word called out to her in a formed her he had something important to show her mentally she was already exhausted the first lady of the generation family wanted to know could it wait but iceberg insisted that she followed him although she was completely exhausted after followed her husband main man to the monitor room it is there that he showed her the disturbing footage of the obsessed Chinese maid, Key Chung.

Ajah, blood began to bold as she watched in complete total shock and rage, she did not know as long as they keep trying with the sick girl who wanted to be her. Key Chung hated her all the same she also was obsessed being with her husband too are you watch kitchen perverted smell and where her under clothes the beach even dancing from the mirror in her lingerie the camera model pause is Iceberg word press the button knowing better than to show anymore footage because then he would be telling on himself and tired baby Sylvester himself would kill him and talk if he knew that the both of them felt he turned in his bed beg your eyes are to say dryly and she whipped on a long single tear away from her face her arms trembled with anger and raised that had taken over her body building up inside of her like a volcano.

"Not a problem boss lady want me to handle that ice eggs paddle his gun on his waist line now there are some things that woman had to handle and there is some things insert and lives of beach shouldn't cross she replied in a bitterly tone as she turned to walk away all Iceberg could do was green from inner ear because he had just told to keep tongue out he already given to the heads up about getting Key Chung taken out before the stupid broad do anything dumb and get him and tie all funked up. Ajah Iceberg loyalty to the family meant more to him than a piece of shit that he could care nothing about to the big fella kitchen was trash someone he and type every black male and use whenever they wanted to for the past few days keychain did sexual favors for him and talk so she could keep her secret safe or she it's so tight it works kinda security monitors until he found ketones relaxing in her bedroom jacuzzi he got ready to enjoy the show.

Strong aroma of marijuana smoke filled the air of the game room area located on the South wing of the Maccin state stop hitting blitz as usual no shirt display in his community tattoos he only had his khaki shorts and his therapeutic stockings on he afterward those staffers because he was a type 2 diabetic who took insulin three times a day that they have helped his blood in his leg circulate better it also helped him prevent blood clots he strongly believed in living fearlessly Thai baby supposed to drink last month but he didn't give a fuck he's still a peanut butter out of the jar already the man wasn't afraid of death it wasn't afraid of diabetic coma either to him he had more immediate concerns like not blowing as high and thinking the clarity when he was high over the years' time baby put in which work in early strikes he was worried about Sylvester his boss and his health so that's the word is ace he will happily die for that old man the man has always treated him like a son despite where he will from Turquoise color Air Force ones were fresh and he had his dreads pulled back into a rough looking ponytail he flipped the flat screen television channels and coughed a blunt smoke. Damn you need to open up a window," Ajah saying it actually sashayed into the green room embarrassing caught by the element of surprise and he nodded in agreement he could tell by the look in her face she was in a foul mood her long hair was pinned up in a sexy way with wisp of her framing her beautiful face but also as he had on sweatpants with some tennis shoes to go along with the all black white beater she wore tightly fitted on her firm breasts I looked down it's going on small workout and going to beat someone asks," what's up my lady how's boss doing Tarbaby double question. "Nothing up but that Chinese slut Sylvester's getting better." she stated in annoyance.

Tar Smiled as he figured out why she was upset it was obvious that iceberg had told her about kitchen foul play a violation." where is that bitch Tar," She asked bitterly the look in his eyes told him he better not play games she was ready to get it popping and very impatient she's in her room I believe you need my assistance my lady he acts no I'm good maybe afterwards she said with the dev list mark as he turned and walked away playing back and forth into sweats time was hypnotized by the Switzerland beauty plump round ass, DAMN, was all he could utter under his breath it is him Jamaican accent as he blew a cloud of smoke out of his nostrils Tarbaby had a thing for the first lady for a while now King John had just gotten out of the jacuzzi and had dried off and wrapped it roll around her body before she laid down and got ready to clean the state tomorrow she wanted to soak she had appetite out of the world as she walked her naked frame only covered by a robe to the refrigerator inside her bedroom it was her very personal small one she had hand on the small door yeah she struck her head into.

What you was looking for in right behind a jug of milk was her leftover bowl of diced pineapples she stretched her arm to reach for it, "BITCH" was all she heard and she felt several blows from a sharp object to the smile and upper part of her back he Chung eyes did to pop out of theirs sockets I told you guys not to talk with me, Ajah screamed as she repeatedly stabbed in the back blow for blow blood is less crowded in Ajah face still in state shock , Key Chung fell to her knees, "No Ajah, No" I just stop I'm sorry I'm sorry shut the FCK up you ain't sorry bitch, Ajah spat. I never was shouting shooting out from over the Chinese made body the cars were help in the screams of agony handsome sided the first lady has somebody lost it and got her first body she would traumatize from all the blood and as she stepped back shaking uncontrollably with a satisfied smile ketones as wide open as a pool of blood began to form from underneath her body, Ajah was out of breath hand me the knife my lady," Tar See it just above a whisper as he and iceberg into the red room iceberg has seen it all on camera in rushed to stop at out of control Ajah, "Hawk spat!" Suspect down until the left out of row she hit a toggle button like it is OK boss lady I clean it up iceberg said as he wrapped his arms around her waist and escorted the traumatized first lady out of the bedroom agile was covered in blood and she did not feel bad about what she had done trying to get her breathing patterns back calm and still waters. Key Chung bell letting disinfect their hurry the right way the girl she thought deserved more than that she felt a little awkward after her first murder as she walked out of the room with Iceberg, she walked away the few drops of Key Chung blood off her face.

"Damn you really fucked up my lady," say it as he covered up what was left of ketone body he crushed down and remove the expensive earrings off of her lifeless body that semester had brought for her 21st birthday you will not need these nos more he stated as he pocket it the earrings and close Key Chung's eyes. tunnel he was the best at ditching bodies, so he looked down at his fresh Air

Force was that now have blood on the bottom bunk man he cursed as he began to roll the body up in a blanket.

Virginia Hospital

Sky patiently instead of next room waiting on Desmond to come back with some food for her in the unborn child she carried Nate was knocked out fast sleep from all the pain medication that the doctors had him on Skype began to drift away to sleep while watching the 11:00 o'clock news she heard the room door cracked openly but thought nothing of it thinking that it was just Desmond returning, "Damn Nigga," he sure took long enough to come back Scott said while I still shut she heard the door close and the sound no response made her open her eyes but when she did she was out of I with the death and she stared down the barrel of the silencer pistol in her face in the full state of shock she wanted to scream but her mouth fell open but nothing came out of it but I liked one the bullet stored through skies little face in his all doc brown janitor staff uniform cycle lead off two shots into skies state of shock face heated his mark between her eyes and in the bridge of her nose and the other shot in the center of her forehead cycle smell to himself because he never killed the person who died mouth and ask open at the same time the sight of it went into his amusement turn around he immediately hit it over to his next emotionless body knowing that he was only on borrowed time. before that he saw walked out earlier return his contract he stood there at the open legs and aim if I had one into the left side of next chest taking Nate out instant with a bullet to the heart next body jerk from the bullet impact bullet is deformed under his hospital gown cycle was the best at his job a true professional at heart when he took shots on his many victims he made sure we can the man has never ever wasted a bullet he knew people were unlikely to live through it below to the heart and to the head or face area. Assassinated people without sacraments living it is how he kept food on his table the Italian men then left out distance shot to the television this guy was watching earlier which now made the room completely pitch black because light was never on in the room damn I hate television he ordered under his breath here's a teacher was drawn to the door when he noticed it opened in the light from the wall it's created to the room yo I knew you ain't had me go get this food and you sleep they stated with all kinds of snacks and sodas for sky and him a plastic bag but now cycle had positioned himself directly behind the door this closed the door and clicked on the switch after guided his hand over the dark wall to find it destroy is the kicked in a little too late after he spotted the television shut out he dropped the plastic bag of snacks and reached for his weapon cycle it out two shots through his silences into the back of Desmond school tend to bring famous out through the front of Desmond forehead in his life his body dropped immediately making his way to the exit end pistol nasty curly tucking his back waist line up he said in his Italian accent I almost forgot the contract said I have he walked over to Skye's lifeless body sending shots into the unborn baby in her stomach.

Chapter Twelve
Toronto Hospital

Damon adds the other hospital showed that after his mother did but his dad up going home with Ajah he went to. I had to submit his father's daily I just had her son that his father had placed him in charge also I told him that his father said he loved him so this is just did not want David to see him so we can help this hey listen headed his way he would not allow Ajah to visit him either. But he couldn't stop her but allowed it is her right to see him because she is his wife smart anger was boiling as he heard every single word his father told them it outside of Sylvester room in that hallway it pays for very deeply that his father didn't want cemented his name if as if he did not even exist his daddy he felt has how do I was in his early teens those days were known smart stay getting kicked out of school and couldn't stop breaking his mother's heart smart stayed in Toronto county jail Ajah would always go bond him out. He said never step foot to see him tears began to trickle down his face at the thought of his dad never showing him though it was always been Sonia this or Damon that Smurf shook his head as he thought about his daddy free gauge out of the South Carolina correctional state prison before he would even free his own son he tried and tried but he could never gain his father's love nor acceptance This is why a couple months after Sylvester got gauge released from prison being jealous and frustrated compels him to get in contact with his father's worst enemy Robert Harris Sr, brainwashed Smurf Smart anything he loved him he also made him believe that he cared it could be a part of the hair of mafia a deal was made for smirk to personally take out his father Robert Harris senior create his powerful tactics down to South Carolina it gets perfectly from prison it was never because of good behavior Smurfs sold out the boy was so naive and dumb to ever think that Robert gave a damn about him Tara being overloaded being mistreated smirk had enough other beats his pop hat with him Smurf stood up out of his seat and stretched before he walked up to one of the goals of generations who got to the door to Sylvester room the guard knew he was not supposed to now no one into the room unless it was first lady Ajah or medical staff. the smart pleaded that he wanted to speak with his dad also that he was worried about his old man the Goon Fucking ass and fell for Smurfs lies Smurf was not sure clear gage Olga had gone. But he was sure the to., The building began to form a large crowd around the decapitated body. NO one knew those to whom the headless body belong. Not even Key Chung's mother and sister knew who body that they were watching. As they too were almost the extremely large nosey crowd. As Toronto city police began to pull up from all different directions.

Maccin Estate

Then we came home to the Maccin state as fast as he could Mama where are you yells get into the kitchen everything the kitchen can have the right open with broken dishes everywhere kitchen looked as if a tornado had hit it was simply ramp side they may finally found his mother after sitting on the floor next to the door crystal too hard knees and hands rocking back and forth with a blank look on her face she looked up at her oldest son he's gone Damon he's going son I just said breaking down again covered her face with both hands as she once again began to cry hysterically it pained me to see his mother now a widow so turn apart she was shaking uncontrollably Damon had never seen his mother look so bad her hair was a hot mess her beautiful brown eyes were red and swollen puffy up to all the clients she had done was it doctor calling her inform her that Sylvester had passed away sometime last night his death has yet to be known he assured add and autopsy report was surely be done to find out what really happens to Sylvester Maccin.

Because Ajah you're the doctor could figure out how the nurse right Sylvester his morning breakfast at 6:30 AM and found the generation boss life is not breathing as you received the devastating news around 7:45 AM surely after iceberg and Todd baby had left the estate first lady Ajah got the call from doctor Roseville the first lady of the Canadian cartoon knew something was terribly wrong because she had left the hospital night before and serviceable to her just fine price all yeah now Sylvester another emotional scar on his heart they will work to his mothers to comfort her he concealed his own emotions knowing he had to be the rock now also Damon knew his mother would need him now more than ever the family will now depend upon him to be strong and be the glue to hold everything together they've been here the heart of a lion and a leader a lot of people couldn't see it in him but he was always warns his expressionless face never showed no kind of anger nor emotions his father Sylvester had left him in charge for a reason mother last semester potential in his oldest son as a matter of fact every member now the roster Sylvester Salas fasting in a small arms around her son back in solving away as she buried her face into his chest and cried uncontrollably they would remain silent as he credited his mother head and held her tight flashbacks of his father invaded his mind and he too dropped a few salad tears I promised my whoever is responsible will pay we must be strong for father he said through gritted teeth.

This is not trust smoke time spoke in his heavy accent name is straight and he does a precautionary measures in all he does but I don't feel he's built for this life we live I said thoughtfully you right man intimidating looks can be deceiving it could be a front man stop at a red light toggle last over iceberg word he must establish trust with us first I don't care if he is against the sun or not a man comes into my life our domain and does not show the proper respect that the food will get aired out our quarterly word beyond bond bro I said it's time baby definitely understood where ice break was coming from my brother we have to respect Sylvester's decision the old man has never misled us in this family we gonna make it man baby this is the spot right here iceberg, pointedly directly ahead.

To the valley blocking Chinatown where he is the best the first picked up key Chung all those years ago iceberg revenge to get the smelly body out of the trunk the sandwich and children playing out in the Miller St heard the rumble of an appear vehicle in the keys scattered like small mice from the sidewalk the children watched on in a huge guy exit the passenger side of the BMW there was a erase Alice in the air as iceberg wanted to the trunk on the vehicle and retrieve the body of ketone as he tossed his steel body onto the clock replacement and if it were a straight piece of trash. The children Chinatown watched in amazement and curiosity more than what the big man had just left on the black large bag in the street the guy jumped into the passenger seat as him in the partner drove down the street the situation was bizarre as the kids ran onto the street to examine the large bag what are the Chinese boys kicked it was only brave one as the other four kids looked on from a distance Open it up one of the five boys yelled scared to do it himself and struggling with this English. The brave would nodded his head in agreement as the brave boy tour and ripped off the bag with a small fingernail he smelled the foul odor first but the continued to rip away until he stumbled backwards following onto his leg Mama one with our children from a five year as them took out running it took the small writing down apartment building the very boy just sat there in the state of shop he was now mentally staring at the heaviest woman body before him he was so afraid of move he wouldn't brave any longer, he realized that he also went himself as well his mother ran out into the morning street and snatched him up he didn't say a word and you could hear the sirens in the distance everyone came out.

Chapter Thirteen
Abandoned Warehouse

"We are one major potential blow away from ending this war we are on the verge of celebration and then my friends victorious" Robert gave his Harold mafia family in warm smile as he adjusts his neck time that matches all Gray suit Robert house singer was literally feeling himself you couldn't tell him that he was in the ship robbing in his head tire mafia had just moved to Toronto ON Canada just three days before Sylvester was killed generation has yet to be informed of the brave power move that Robert Harold senior had done. some of Robert Harris men felt like the move was not brave but stupid and also suicidal definitely after killing Sylvester Maccin. shoot the entire Canadian cartel would surely want Robert blood Robert also wanted to see more of Amanda he mid weeks ago but no one apart of Harold mafia would ever challenge Robert Harrell senior's decision making I completely agree boss the momentum is clearly on our side first the daughter of Sylvester, Ajah Sonia Maccin and then Desmond his brother Nate then finally the head of their organization. Suggest some hacking himself is now gone I will say job well done." as Canon stated. as he leaned back in his comfortable chair surrounded the conference table Drayton Bruce set also at the large table silently taking in everything that was being said I called this meeting for the four of us to come to a conclusion about Smurf Sylvester was his very own father and the board didn't give a damn about selling him out Roberts stated taking a seat at the conference table allowing his words to marinate in the minds of the three most trusted men cannon Drake and Bruce.

I personally think about that we should put him to sleep at the bottom of the Lake Ontario," Bruce was first to voice his opinion at the large table. "I totally agree with Bruce on loyalty is unacceptable in my book the boy's old out his family, "Drew said as he shook his head in disgust he hated folks who traded size for any reason healed ray loved the NBA and highlight disagreed when LeBron left Cleveland the man simply felt you win with your team and you died and suffer with your team point blank no questions about it. "Very wealthy and can in my man it's not to say your input doesn't count but the vote is 3 to one already or 40 because I believe Dre and Bruce are definitely right Smurf Maccin deserves to die." Robert Harold stated. just like his father if not worse the both of them are about that life all I can say is good luck." with that said the Muslim brother walked on out of the conference room leaving a nervous Robert Harold with just his own thoughts of some regrets.

Lake Ontario 11:49pm

Olga and Gauge Set it apartments in complete silence watching the stars together on the late-night Canada sky as a cool breeze off of the Lake Ontario blue fairway gauge places arms around August shoulder and pulled her closer to keep her warm. Ajah seriously hurt by the loss of her boss and also mentor friend and a father figure the loss of Sylvester was taken a serious toll on her she took it extremely hard just like the first lady Ajah Maccin. "Gauge Baby do you believe what Damon said she questioned about what ma Damon said a lot of things in that meeting he replied I'm talking about saying he believes murphy was behind their father's death it's a strong possibility I mean the boy has been acting very strange as of late even before his father filed death I wouldn't put it past him he shrugged his shoulders knowing he thought of and felt the same way that Damon did. Gauge had lived in a cell with Smurf and he knew when the boy was troubled doctors claim he had another heart attack a massive one this time but Sylvester was fine when Ajah left that night she told me he was going to get some rest medical staff had advanced it so something or someone brought this bullshit on, Olga August said in a hurtful tone one thing for sure I will bring down Robert Harris senior and that water down the Harold mafia gaze lifted her chin so he could see her face see that's the problem I disagree with David orders for you to go in undercover and get close to Robert Harrell senior those people are real mom before he could continue ogre jumped to her feet and I'm for real gauge I've been the hitwoman for generation for years no one is as good as me she stared down at gauge with a cloudy vision the pain of her mentor death was killing her inside she saw the gauge was getting upset so she lowered her tone and cleared her throat" baby I understand that you are concerned about my safety but I'm a big girl and you gotta let me do this on my own and alone trust me I'm not a rookie." all I know that you're not green to this kind of stuff he said standing at first Murph was reluctant to come to the funeral but his mother begged for him to come but pay his respects to his own father I've never once saw the distant look behind her younger sons eyes Smurf was one they had her current pain and she had no clue he knew if his mother found out that she would hate in this own him for life As for his brother Damon and the rest of the Canadian cartel he knew if they was to find out that that would be the end of his life there was no doubt in his mind about that at all like track and field it would be a racer who put a bullet in his head first no explanations and no excuses.

The Aftermath- Conference

"With all due respect Dona Anderson, I've won the war inside the little problem don't answer Sylvester Maccin I am tired of your nagging Anderson I did what I had to do Robert Harold senior shouted as he rose to his feet from the conference table surrounded by bosses so he could lock eyes with Don Anderson who was sitting directly across the table in front of him why so angry my friend this is your beef not none of ours Don Anderson replied also correction I am not nagging but simply letting you know that you haven't won shit. I was there at Sylvester funeral upon giving David in the mechanic a manly handshake he removed his shades and all I saw was hate and revenge he assured me he will finish where his father left off and you Robert will die he said upon down errors or last statement Robert had a single began to sweat in a small lump formed in his throat as it became hard for him to swallow his own spit he tried to hide his fear but the smell was too much fake. I am not worried about Damien Mac in the head of the snake Sylvester is six feet under. "Excuse me", Don Eljar cleared his throat you are truly a fool Robert Harold you never underestimate no man hell even a faggot born with balls you take away the boy father and thinks shit sweet then your disrespect by moving to Toronto on generation home turf don Eljar shook his head in disbelief I'm going back to Texas to prepare for your funeral old friend." Eljar still it to his feet and excused himself. Moonja was a man of few words but he to believe that Robert Harris singer was very foolish he too stood to leave, "Sao Akhir you feel the same way they do?" Moonja stopped in his tracks without turning around, "why yes, Damon Maccin, word is not no slow leak although he may not look it that boy is popping. Damon circle his brother walking around, as if he was it's not shark going in a circle around his prey poor Smurf lay down on the floor bought up in a fetal position crying like a newborn baby he was barely beaten and busted up he could only see out of one eye tar baby the iceberg had hailed him in position while Damon took out his anger and pain on Smurf. as his brother circled him in a trance and zone Smurf had never seen him and before tar baby and iceberg still not too far away from an action as both of them will serve hurricane Damon for Tom maybe he was in deep thought that thinking did Smurf village you what his brother said he did Smurf had yet to admit and own up to his wrongdoing tar baby always like Smurf and had a strong bond with the kid he was ready to jump in and end the misery that the poor boy was going through shoot after all he had never even saw Smurf kill a fly let alone picking up his first body who by the way is his own father but Tom baby did not want to question Damon instincts he allowed it to play out" Ughh, Fuck" Smurf scream in agony as he held on to his midsection Damon had drilled his size 11 boots straight into the stomach of his own flesh and blood. "Enough playing around coward I know it was you who killed father, "Damon shouted incomplete race sweating profoundly and now his 9-millimeter aimed at Smurfs head, "Fuck you, Damon." You are the Coward!" 'Yeah, he shouted was me who took the old bastard out. He never loved me, he only cared for Sonya and you." Smurf could barely speak as he was now crying uncontrollably Damon kept his gun aimed as he now also was dropping tears of his own even the two killers of tar and Berg were getting cloudy vision from the confessional Smurf before Damon could get a word out of his mouth Ajah burst through the office doors, "so because you were jealous Smurf you break my heart and kill your own father!" her eyes puffy and swollen but there was no tears this time. Ajah Maccin look at her once favorite son will disgusting hate Damon had told her to not enter the room no matter what he promised he would make Smurf confess and true to his word that this is what happened but Mama I was smack it's Mercedes was cut off by August hand you not my son I saved you all your life," she sobbed. I cannot save you this time with that being said she turned and walked out the room. "BOOM"

Ajah stopped outside in the hallway as she broke down knowing she last another child.

Chapter Fourteen
Buffalo NY

A true Muslim his faith never waver in he embraced all knowledge Moonja was a peaceful brother and he stayed faithful to the Nation of Islam he always had small parties a lot of his friends and business associates could get together for the most part Moonja just wanted to create peaceful areas for the women and children in every state but he knew that there was a lot of work and almost impossible so he just tried to keep as many safe and possible from the violence in the world his party consisted of people from all walks of life from monsters and the cartel organizations and it times leaders of different St gangs Moonja plan was always bring together those who didn't get along and shared some positive light into whatever negative situation that they had going on. Plain and simple Moonja wanted to bring an end to the awards and balance along the entire East Coast he had done and exceptional well job in the South helping brothers come together to get money without shooting up the projects and neighborhoods where a lot of women and children lived that is why he was not holding this party in his hometown of Winston Salem NC.

Moonja wanted to bring peace to Buffalo NY the place where Harold mafia had once lived but still controlled the area all drugs that came through the city didn't get sold unless Harold himself located the party was live and everyone was having a good time." look all I'm saying my brother is do not count generation out that is still a dangerous family Moonja warned as he studied Robert Harold eyes the herald mafia boss was not even paying attention to moon word of wisdom Monday track but turned around to see what had caught his friend attention and justice Moonja had figured it was a woman but none as he had seen before the beautiful woman sat at the bar cross legged sipping on her third drink at the bar there was no shame in her game at all she was in a heated stare down with Robert Harold her legs shined from being well oiled up she had a short cut hair style which was entered the girl from GI Jane and her dress shirt threatened to rise up her thick thighs and hips unfold nouned Robert knew her damn you caught himself saying I bet she has no panties Roberts said take the last sip of his drink no Big Brother you know that goes against what I stand for but I do believe you are right on that statement by her I would say she's not your normal white woman she doesn't look to be from our country well how about I find out Moonja my brother Robert smiled as he handed moon you're his empty glass and headed out for the direction of the seductive beauty queen. August Madden licked her lips ducks seductively as she watched her prey head over towards her Robert Harold was falling into her trap and she did not know it but, in his case, he was falling into her spider web and the guy was sure to be tangled up she had told him she may come to the party.

Chapter Fifteen

Ajah Maccin was awakened from her beauty rest by a knock on her bedroom door. With dried up cold built in her eyes and a cotton mouth. She yawned as she clutched onto her new husband under her pillow a revolver handgun, she had not been taken care of herself much as she smelled like a skunk just sprayed her for the past few weeks the first lady of the Canadian cartel had been showering once a week and not eating much she felt as if she was not only losing her mind but losing her soul as well/

the family she had was now torn apart her husband she loved so was now gone and Sonia was too but to top it all off Smurf who was her favorite of all her children he was now dead by the hands of her eldest son Damon Smurf took away her soulmate in heart Sylvester now will never grow old with her and they wouldn't even watch their first grandchild birth tears rolled down her face onto the warm pillow.

"Knock, Knock, Knock!

coming into Yale the harvest mail almost knocked my baby off of his feet when he opened the bedroom door it did not bother Archer because she was immune to it he tried not to gag my lady Damon called and said do you need him to hire A new made no I am good tar she replied with her back towards him lying in a fetal position.

the quiet sellers told her that tar baby was once again watching her as she knew he had liked her and had feelings for her too before she could tell him to leave her alone he broke the awkward silence piece my lady it is none of my business but look mom I'm not going to let you go out like this you are still first lady and still beautiful too he wasn't sure if he overstepped boundaries Audrey couldn't do nothing but blush she hadn't smiled in months Audrey was glad to her back with this man. I don't what you be miserable my lady he says standing in the doorway why do you care she asks finally to turn around in the bed to face him top baby broke eye contact as he looked down to the floor with this loyalty comes consequences mom and for what reason mom I cannot say he lifted his head back up to a smile Ajah knew he wanted her. he also really cared for her so now get your *** up and go wash my lady he ordered with a light green of his own yes Sir Mr. tar I just said granted herself he turned around to leave history is hanging freely where may I ask are you going she quizzed tonight mom Robert Harris singer dies Olga was see to it and I must go get the helicopter ready malady he stated in his Jamaican accent finally yes good make sure he's dead add replied with much hate in her eyes and voice no doubt mom we got you he nodded his head oh and I'll have you some loud pack skunk weed rolled up when you returned now you talking he grinned as they both laughed a little before a time baby closed the door he was making his way into her damaged heart.

Chapter Sixteen

Guage at in the wooden chair his hands tied together behind the chair unable to break free started to hyperventilate and feel dizzy he was weak from Robert Harris senior forced some kind of liquid down his throat against his will he had been savagely beaten by two of Roberts goons Bruce and Dre.

Guage helplessly watched on as Olga the love of his life lay face down barely breathing Bruce and ray had pistol whipped her like a rag doll. Unable to hold his own head up Robert singer health gauge head up by lifting his chin while roaring in laughter seeing Mr. Guage this is the consequences you pay when you cross me and kill my son and grandbaby finish that Bitch," Bruce he ordered in pure rage "no problem boss", Bruce praised the 38 Special against the back of her skull no gay shouted in tears " Boom"

The CBC News was playing on the television as a volume was at Max Gage awoke in an ice cold sweat as he looked around the room for any signs of Olga the two little birds have been together all day in the motel room making love Damon had forbid that the two of them saw one another after the Robert junior hit at the hospital just today before but gauge listened to orders Robert Harris senior son had been dead for a while over 24 hours and his body had yet to be found Needless to say that Robert Harris senior had no idea about his oldest son and grand babies death gates had no clue as to Olga had done undercover to lure Robert senior in. Gaze was already skeptical about the tags before Olga in a few hours to take down Robert Harris senior alone he saw that all of August clothes were gone and he instantly knew where she snuck off to he shook his head in total disbelief because he couldn't believe she didn't wake him up before she left to go kill Robert senior but he also understood why she didn't wake him he would have tried to convince her to let him accompany her gates had been given over his word not to get involved and let her handle it the bad dream he just awoken from now had him second guessing his decision he had already lost his own father and best friend he did not want to lose the woman he planned on making his wife he looked at his watch and the time read 10:08 PM he hopped out of the bed in his boxes and white T shirt. When he looked on the nightstand where he expected his car keys to be at, he saw that Olga had stolen his keys and left a note in place of them he sat on the bed and read slowly to himself.

antibiotics let me be all you need and more so wait please don't close the door I know a woman have hurt you you're bleeding from your wounds let me save you from your doom so you are so you won't catch a disease let me help you breathe show that I'm all unique scars over your heart has caught in their fiction I'm your antibody allow me to love you back into the right direction your wings are healing so never let our love change with the seasons if I've ever hurt you then please forgive me just know it wasn't intentionally because I'll suffer 1000 days before I allow you to suffer one to leave the past cause what's done is done no more excruciating pain no more sad songs you sang plus your past down the drain your love now in my domain reciprocate in my arms baby this is where you belong barricaded yourself inside my heart now look around there's a lot of light after dark open your eyes you're alive yes I've nurse you back to health hallucinate not baby boy this woman never left antibiotics a poem by Olga AKA your love

Guage quickly got himself together before he could even shed a tear the big fella always enjoyed her poems ogre loved her write them all the time although the woman was a cold blooded killer she also had a soft side as well he knew that he brought emotions and feelings out of her that no other man has ever done although he was very proud of making her fall in love with him he also knew that love could make you weak cloud your judgment and get you unfocused he knew because he was now suffering from the effects of love Guage refused to let Olga slip and mess up this mission by being unfocused she could not lose her life because of him he faded the small piece of paper and stood to his feet in search of his clothes.

Chapter Seventeen
Saint Augustine FL Club Might Dollars

Saint Augustine Fl. Club Mighty Dollars Club Mighty Dollars was literally Jumping out of the Gym from every Single Angle. The Strip Club was always like. But tonight, everyone was in the building celebrating the Birthday Party For one of their best Strippers, MS Thickness. Everyone and their momma were in the building Tonight Ms. Thickness did not dance, she was fully dressed, celebrating her 19th Birthday, Her Daddy was a notorious king Pin to the city. But She never respected him for killing people and Selling drugs. So, she did not stay connected much. The girl Shared an apartment with her Co. worker Diamond, who had yet to make her grand entrance Ms. Thickness father was on his way to the club, so he could celebrate with his only Child, although he did not like her occupation. He still loved his daughter and hoped one day she world allow him to take care of her and quit the degrading Stripper Job, outside the club Just a couple blocks away. Death was on the Horizon.

Back IN Toronto Canada 10:36 PM

Thank God for Spare key, He Whisper to self, Gauge Speed through Red light after Redlight, hoping that a police squad car would not spot him. He was rushing to the aid of his soulmate Olga; He maneuvered his Benz in and out of traffic. Switching Lanes as if he were fast and the Furious his damn self. Gauge destination was The CN Tower. He knew he was breaking his word to Olga. But he could not allow her to handle this alone. He did at give a flying Fur What Damon Ordered. The Sounds of Jay-Z Voice blasted through speakers

Cars As he nodded his head to the beat of Death of Auto

Southern American Wilaya was totally focus on one thing And That was laying down any and everyone who tried to harm his Queen. If he lost his life behind her. Then it was what It was He no longer the old felt that he owed Sylvester His life. Because indebted to Olga for American man was dead, but now Gauge felt he was his life New Meaning. He was only tour blocks away. when he received his eyes off of the road only momentarily, Gauge open message Box to Fine a text from His love, He smiled to no himself as he read it, I am on the way to the mark saying estate the words over meet me their babe the helicopter would be landing in about 30 minutes love you. guys through the phone into the passion seat as he broke a Kool aid smile. he hit a 360 turn in the middle of the night highway as he now was heading to the Maccin estate to meet his woman.

Back at the Might Dollars

just a few blocks away iceberg and Damon sat patiently in their ride intelligence had given them he is up about Robert al single last strip club down in St Augustine FL so instead of heading back to north after the death of Canon in South Carolina Damon and iceberg just stuck around in the South just a little while longer. "I will just text mission complete the wars over Damon said proudly to ice the two men dapped up in a victory handshake. Earlier that day I swear had planted C fours losses all around the building of club mighty Dallas when nobody was around the area" you had to finish this job boss?" iceberg questioned as he continued to smile with the detonator in his right hand "set it off, bro let's go home." Damon said as he cranked up the ride and emerging to the late night traffic iceberg waited until the both of them was in safe distance away from the club before he pressed the button which sent the entire club into a blaze the massive explosions had a thunderous loud sound as a breeze and went up in the air a huge fireball lit up the nightly sky where club minded dollars once existed the war was officially over with the Harold mafia so versus death was finally avenge because ogre made sure that the bad thing about the end of this war was that unbeknownst to generation a new war had just begun Joel generations intelligence had informed Damon that club might have dollars belonged to Robert Harrell senior but what he did not tell Damon was that Don Anderson daughter miss thickness also known as Tammy worked at the club and now all heard 19 birthday she was dead in a horrible death her father was only minutes away from the disaster and pain he would suffer once he found out about his only child.

Epilogue

Little Jamaican Boy heard a loud crashing Sound as He Awoke out of his In and out Sleep, He was on tender age of fourteen and wherever He smoked Weed with his father, Tarzan then ger always overshadow the heavy Eyes.

of Sleep he felt showring over him. He was not afraid to go Check It out. AS Tarzan got up off of his bed, He dragged his feet in his Rugrats pjs. As soon as He reached the threshold to his bedroom door Pop, Pop, Popp! Noor, He heard His mother Scream, As the Hallway was pitch Black except for the light flashing from the weapons fired, Tarzan had no weapon. But His father had taught Him how to use gauge very well for his age, unbeknownst to him of how many Intruders there was in there home And Clueless as to what to do S ran to his closet and hid underneath the dirty clothes His mother had yet to laundry. He made sure to cover himself well. As the Shots Continue to be heard from down the hallway of his parents' bedroom

When suddenly there were no more Screams non cries for mercy. He never heard His father, but young Tarzan was sure that his father fought back because of the small was of gurus blasting. Soon He Heard footsteps, not mowing who had Entered his room until he heard the language of Chinese men Tarzan could not make out what They were saying. But it was obviously they were more than upset? He could hear the mess trashing His room. Breaking Things, when suddenly an AK-47 sculpted, it made the boy heartbeat Even harder out of His Chest. He knew his gun's well, and He was she as to the weapon He now heard. Fluids were & Whereas Sweat poured Profusely from his young body from being underneath.

the Extremely hot dirty clothes. As well as the tears that poured down Tarzan Young "Face because He was Elise his parents were no longer alive. He laid in a fatal position shivering, not because it was cold. But from now being Afraid of what the Chinese men man do to him now, unbeknownst to Young Tarzan He had an iso Pee on Himself. Suddenly the rampage of bullets Stopped. He made out one of the men.

language and saying stopped the let us go. The weird footsteps were not the tears that poorer.

He laid in a fare because He was sure no longer. Tarzan waited only a few minutes to come from out of 25 Hiding as He held onto mushed like It was a baseball bat ready to Swing for the fences. Shaking for uncontrollably long Tarzan made his way down the Eerie dark hallway, Never In his 14 years of living had he been this scared out of his mind. He knew his father had run and brought his family with him from Jamaica when He was only nine years old. Because of the money He owed the Chinese. So, To Dodge the Triade Tarzan father Demarcus relocated His family to the States to the city of Rochester New York, not too far from Buffalo N4, upon entering His parents' bedroom the Scene was something out of a horror film. As his mother laid totally spiral Across their bed In Her all-black night gown with half of her face blown off, one Eye still Open and some of her brain missing, Seller Shots to

Tarzan Her torso, As Young throwed-up all over the floor from the sight and the foul order of blood and death. He ran out of the room dropping the mushy A little further down the Hallway to the kitchen. He spotted His father Shirtless in His Jean's laid out face first to the floor. Demarcus long dreads covered his face as. He had several holes In His Back, with His Glock not too far from Him on the floor Tarzan picked up the bun with Tears.

flowing as He sobbed. He had a mixture of Pain, Guilt and hate. The Pain because Although He never respected His father Grimes His Cowardly Acts. The man still had showed him a lot, especially a with handling weapons. The Guilt because He felt like he coward out like Did when he fled Jamaica Because His momma was Innocent and she media

The only two males In Her life and Although He was young Tarzan felt he Could had done something. She cried out for her life, and He hid In the Closet like a little boy. At that moment he decided to never feel such shame and disgrace again. The Hate He felt was towards the man who laid before Him. The man who borrows People's money and spend It on Hoes and his wonderful mother. The man who If He'd honor Cheating at his word, maybe Still have His home To Tarzan surprised His father rolled over on His background Tarzan in Pain my son Call for Help" Demarcus mouth. Tarina stood utter through over Him Clutching

a bloody Filled has no Bullet.

the block with no more Tears. The In his front coward probably was running Again? Tarzan thought to Himself. Young Tarzan Took Two Steps Closer to words is.

"Who child Are you Boy? "Sylvester grilled. Never Allowing the Boy to

Turn Around with His Eyes He gave Iceberg a disappointed gaze, my parents are Dead, I Just Wanted some money, Eye. Please save me a chance mom Tarzan Begged, as He began to Sob, feeling like

Sylvester put his gun Away and Turned the kid Around, holding bother of His Shoulders. Looking Down to The Dark-Skinned boy. CA Real man works for His living Sun, do you want a Job? Sylvester asked, before Tarzan could Answer, Sylvester could search his eyes, and could Ten this Boy would be loyal That he would not regret this but on the end, He saw Aman dressed sharp and smooth. A man without saying oozed power and wealth. He did not know what Ima of business Sylvester into on He and the big guy line was of

Profession. But he would soon find out that this would be his Family until his dying Day, In Sylvester's Eye's radiated Security, Strength and Also danger. But the positive dangers If such a thing After that night The Boy never looked back, under Sylvester leadership He learned how to fly a plane, and a helicopter. He also learns how to really be a stone-cold Killer. Sparing no one at alle His mother Always said I named you tur291, because although are not white You Brave like the guy in the movie. But as a same King your black AS Tar. He despised that name felt that night allowing His mother to die. He was Anything but brave.

Tarzan because he So He Charged. His name to TAR BABY. "Shit? Tarbaby awoke next to Ajah Maccin in a cold Sweat He felt Wrong in Her bed where the man He respected so once laid his head. Yes, He had feelings for Ajah but There were many Demons He had to deal with first before he focusses on Anyone else No Tarbaby Didn't had sex with her, But He Instead held her and comfort her. Without Question He was Attracted to her what wrong Tarbaby You okay? She awakes could tell he had a bad dream.

cons hang your black a Brave the then you arch. Sparing niche felt that nock As Tar. He the guy in them because altered at all. o He is changing allowing His past that name it. But as ought you

His body washed down In Sweat

I gotta go. I Check on via tomorrow may warehouse extend.

Dad, who was obviously In Pain and Agony! Sure, like you help family Momma? He raised the gun Aimed Steady at his own father's head. No longer was He Shaker like a leaf. Boy What Are you doing? His father manages to utter while coughing up dark blood. DeMarcus had never saw his son so calm, focus and face made of stone.

"I'm Being A man?" Tarzan Squeezed the trigger, Sending a round directly Into His father forehead. AS Tarzan sighed walked out if the house lost

One week later

Tarzan had been staying hidden from the authorities. He understood the police had found those bodies and had plenty of Questions as to was He was Dead or Alive. Also, He did not want to be found insure as to if the Chinese would come back and finish the Job of his life for his father's sin or to be found and then placed in a faster care system, so in desperate need of a hot bath and some food. Tarzan notice a Gas Station one night; it was well late After 3 am In the morning. He had just come from out of his hidden spot in an old Abandon Junkies house. He was homeless and desperate. Need to say losing an His youth watching Every Night People hooting up drugs and prostitutes get their backs blown out, Hello ma can you spare some change man? upon hearing the young Boys Accent, The Big fella could tell the boy was not American nor

Canadian Iceberg reach Into His pocket pulled out a Five-dollar bill He had just step out of the SUV to pump gas. When Young Tarzan saw the wad of money. He pulled out His father's.

"Give me all you got!" He timed at Big Ice Chest, never looking I see who saw him, you really wanna do this kid? Iceberg Asked mad that He got caught slipping being serve nous

Do nodded his head in a gesture to say yes. This was when He felt Sylvester Chrome Revolver press to the back of His skull. Tarzan was frozen in time. As He handed the Coven to Iceberg

*Two weeks Later South Beach * * ***

It Is not what the eye can see that brings me Pride. But the warm and caring person you are deep down inside.

It is your gentle Strength, your laughter, the Joy you always give. your honesty and kindness, and the thoughtful wait you live.

What makes you So Special right from the very start? It is the most important thing of all the love That's in your heart!

Love you, love you still, always have, always will Love your wife Olga.

(What makes you Special! Poem)

Gauge Smiled, as he finishes listening to the Sweet Poem

Gauge smiled as he finish listening to the sweet poem that his newly wed wife Olga read off the small piece of paper, The two of them had just eloped just two days earlier and was now joying a romantic Honeymoon down in Miami Florida, Gauge Stood with his large frame directly behind her, His massive arms wrapped ever so around Olga's curvaceous Body. They Both stared off into the ocean Sun began to set in the distance of South Beach Miami Florida o told him that she did not kill Robert and Naomi Baby, But Gauge had Charmin too I love you Gauge, Olga Said in a low sweet tone. I know Ma and I too, He replied, she turned around in his arms, so that both looking face to face, Gauge never once breaking their embrace, as their lip locked in a heated passionate kiss. As the two of them stood on the sand enjoying one of the greatest gift's lives has to offer, Real Love

THE END!

Questions

1. Who was your favorite character and why?

2. After Olga Informed Damon the War was over, Do You Think He should not had blown up Robert Harold Sr Club mighty Dollars?

3. Do you feel like Sylvester Was a Boss or A Bully?

Do you feel Nate was the cause of cause Sonya's death by not protecting her but allowing love to cloud his focus on the Job?

3. Why Do You Think Olga Allowed Robert Harold Jr child to Stay Alive?

4. How Do you Rate This Novel 1 To 10, and 10 being highest?

5. Is This your favorite Jay Phoenix novel?

6. Do You Think Aja his next maid should be a man?

7. Do You Think Gauge made Olga soft?

8. Did Sylvester left Generation. In Good hands with Daman?

9. Did you Think Tan Baby and Iceberg was wrong for Selling.

10. What would you like to see In Part Two?

13.) Ladies If you were Ajah Maccin, how would you have handled Key Chung? Key Chung Out After Getting What They wanted?

14.) Is Ajah wrong for Flirting with tar Baby?

Don't miss out!

Visit the website below and you can sign up to receive emails whenever Jay Phoenix publishes a new book. There's no charge and no obligation.

https://books2read.com/r/B-A-QJCU-UGIZB

BOOKS2READ

Connecting independent readers to independent writers.